The Pieces of Us

DANIELLE LATRICE

D1599933

DANIELLE
Latrice

For permission requests, inquiries can be sent to info@daniellelatrice.com.

Books may be purchased for educational, business, or sales promotional use. For information, please email info@daniellelatrice.com.

Printed in the U. S. A.

First Printing, March 2021.

Library of Congress Cataloging-in-Publication Data has been applied for.

ISBN: 978-1-953156-33-4

DEDICATION

To my grandmother Carol, who always encouraged me to reach for the stars.

ACKNOWLEDGMENTS

Most importantly, I would like to thank God. Without you, I wouldn't have possessed the strength and courage to accomplish any of this. While working on this book, I kept Jeremiah 29:11 scripture close to me as a reminder. A reminder to let go of control and follow your lead in the plan you'd designed for me. I am so grateful that you trusted me with this gift and I pray that you bless me with many more days and opportunities to walk in my purpose.

Shaundrika Knight, thank you for the abundant amount of support that you have provided throughout this writing process and in our friendship. If it wasn't for your persistent encouragement to return to my writing, I might not be standing here now with a completed book. I could never thank you enough for being one of my biggest cheerleaders.

Kanta Cadogan, thank you for being such a moving force in my life. You have been so graceful in how you've encouraged me to prevail and understand my light. You've always held me accountable and have inspired me to walk my path of healing and self-discovery. I am so thankful that God allowed us to cross paths.

Jimmy Pierce, thank you for being such an incredible mentor. You have been so influential in my journey of growth and have guided me in so many decisions. Your patience, wisdom, and kindness created a positive and nurturing space where I could share and learn from you. I can only hope that I am able to be such an impactful person to someone else, as you have been to me.

Irma Ingram and Shishova Cheatham, thank you for being a consistent source of support as I navigated through the many life experiences that left emotional scars and impacted my storytelling. You were always readily available with love and kindness, to which I will always be thankful.

Chantel Foxhall, thank you for encouraging me to push through when my faith seemed slippery. Bruce Wayne is here to stay, RT!

Kiara Foxhall, my twin, your fearless drive to pursue your entrepreneurial dreams has left seeds of inspiration. I deeply appreciate your unwavering support. Kisses!

Shalonda Batten, thank you for being the yin to my yang. Much of what I've experienced that birthed this book, you were there to hold me up. I am so happy to currently be experiencing a life that you spoke into existence then.

To my parents, family, and friends, I cannot express enough gratitude for the limitless amount of support and love that you have provided. In many ways, the relationships that I've shared with you have molded my foundation in some manner and will continue to be an important essence of who I am. I hope that I can continue to make you proud. Love you!

TABLE OF CONTENTS

FRIENDSHIP IS HEALING FOR THE SOUL

D.L.

LOCKS

A good friend can be compared to the stars. Even when they are not visible, your heart knows that they are there.

— D.L.

Whether we know it or not, our lives are bound together and connected through an unseen tapestry of experiences. Unbeknownst to us, every passing hour and every passing day, we make the decision to pick up pieces and place them back down in hopes that they fit precisely into the greater puzzle that shapes and molds our lives. It is in this act that we seek interconnectedness with the people, places and things in the world around us, the greatest of all sentiments rooted in companionship. The by-product of companionship can only be discovered amidst the grasp of friendship. Over the years and through unprecedented trial and tribulation, Desirae, Jennifer and Ashlee simultaneously taught each other by merit and by deed the true essence of sisterhood. Unquestionably the personification of grit and persistence, they were the girls who resolved to get up when they fell. They created castles from the stones that were thrown their way and constructed walls from the ashes of pain and the dust of prosperity. Through it all, they never managed to lose sight of their connection even amidst life's most turbulent times. In the end, they would come to realize that the smaller pieces became the construct of the bigger picture.

CHAPTER 1

LOOP

Desirae

Lucid Dreams

It was 5 a.m., and the alarm clock was insistent on not allowing Desirae to sleep any longer. She arose with what felt like the weight of the world on her shoulders and pushed back the covers just enough to release her from the hold of the sheets. Peeling herself from the bed, she lifted her arms into the air. Stretching in a desperate attempt to prepare for the day ahead, she let out a sigh. In a trance-like state, she placed one foot in front of the other until she reached the archway of her bedroom door. She peered out into the humble hallway and paused for a moment before walking toward the bedroom nearest to hers. Still halfway asleep, she reached for the knob and turned the handle to enter.

Upon entrance, she walked to the bed, revealing two younger boys with features that mirrored hers. She reached to slightly nudge the one closest to the edge of the bed, saying, "Wake up." To no avail. She repeated herself. "Wake up, Ethan."

He replied, "No, leave me alone."

Desirae nudged him harder, this time with the conviction of an older sister, and said, "Wake up right now, Ethan, and go brush your teeth. It's time to get ready for school."

Eventually, he sat up as she repeated the same sequence with the other boy. "Zachary, wake up. It's time for school." Once she managed to wake them both, they stumbled out of bed and walked to the door with Desirae following closely behind to ensure their safety.

In true supervisory fashion, Desirae stood behind them as they began to brush their teeth, shortly thereafter reaching for her toothbrush to attend to her own. "When you're done, go get dressed and meet me downstairs for breakfast. Your uniforms are on the handle of your closet door."

They nodded in agreement, and Desirae retreated to her bedroom to begin her ritual of getting dressed.

By the time Desirae made her way to the kitchen, both brothers, still in a state of slumber, were slumped in their chairs with their heads atop the table. Desirae walked over to the cupboard and reached for two bowls, which she filled with cereal and a small amount of milk. The sound of her placing the bowls and spoons on the table startled one brother, causing him to sit up. She reached to lift the head of the other brother, who was still asleep, saying, "Hurry and eat. You cannot miss the bus."

"But I'm not hungry," he replied. Knowing that he would need something in his stomach to get through the day, she replied, "Eat anyways. You'll be hungry by the time you get to school."

After they finished, Desirae escorted the boys to the front door and stood on the front porch watching them walk safely down the driveway and over two houses to the bus stop. Once they were secured on the bus, Desirae went back inside to finish getting prepared for the day.

After pulling her hair into a ponytail and putting on her shoes, she grabbed her backpack from the chair next to her bed and exited the room, closing the door behind her. She walked back down the hallway until she reached the third door, where she knocked timidly and waited for a response. A soft whimper came from the other side of the door: "Come in."

Desirae took a deep breath and slowly opened the door, peeking her head in before fully entering. The room was dark, and a person lay hidden under the covers. Desirae took a few steps into the room, stopping well before the bed.

"Mom, I'm leaving. The boys are already gone for school."

"Okay baby, have a good day." Her voice was muffled from under the covers.

"I will. Are you going to get out of bed today?"

"Oh, don't you worry about me. Just go to school. I'll be here when you get back."

Desirae turned and walked back to the door, stopping and turning slightly to glimpse her mother settling back into bed. "Okay, I love you," she whispered before closing the door.

In Real Time

The roaring sound of the alarm clock forced Desirae to flee from the lucid dream of her childhood and back into the reality of the day ahead. Now at 30 years old, her childhood seemed like a distant memory. After stretching to turn off the ruckus, she retrieved her phone from atop the nightstand and plunged back into the sea of pillows to stare at the ceiling. Eventually, she began checking her messages, noticing that she had missed several text messages after falling asleep abruptly.

The first text was from Samantha, her assistant. *Good morning Ms. Sanders. Just a reminder that you have a prospective client meeting this morning at 10:00 am. Mr. Richardson called and requested that we confirm as soon as possible.*

To which she replied: *Okay. I'll be in the office by 9:00 am.*

She slid to the next unopened text from Ashlee. It read *Girl's night next weekend, my house.*

Desirae smiled to herself before typing, *Good with me.*

Eager and with anticipation, she sat up before sliding to the next text from Malik, which read, *I need to see you. When are you free?*

Without hesitation, she responded, *I'm flexible after this week. Are you coming here?*

Three bubbles appeared on the phone almost immediately. *Naw, I'm going to have you meet me in Miami. Let's shoot for the last weekend.*

I can make that work, Desirae typed back with a smirk.

I'm going to send you the money to book your flight and get something to wear. You know how I like to see you.

Desirae responded with a heart emoji before placing the phone back on top of the nightstand and peeling herself from the bed to walk into the bathroom.

Now standing in front of the sink, she turned on the cold water and began to splash her face in an attempt to be fully present. After drying her face with the towel on the stand atop the counter, she began to closely examine her face in the mirror, turning her head to the left and scrutinizing her side profile. She stepped back to allow more of her body to be seen in the mirror as she worked to love the reflection.

She took a deep breath before the multitude of Post-It notes that she had written and placed all over the mirror over the past few months came into focus. The notes were filled with affirmations and sayings that she needed to be reminded of from time to time. Taking it all in, she removed her robe and observed herself a little closer. Now wearing only a fitted tank and panties, she could see herself fully. Desirae skimmed over the Post-It notes once more and let out a deep sigh before reading two aloud.

"I deserve to be happy.
I am enough."

With that confirmation, she walked back into her bedroom to get dressed for the day before going downstairs to prepare breakfast for herself.

The walk down the extended hallway was a reminder of the hard work she had exerted over the years. The walls revealed several degrees and certifications, all a reflection of her accomplishments. Seeing her name etched onto the documents reinforced that she deserved everything that she had and all that she intended to work to attain.

She heard white noise as she approached the living room and remembered that she'd left the TV on accidentally before heading upstairs for bed. When she arrived downstairs, she walked to the couch to retrieve the remote to turn it off and noticed that the early morning news was reviewing several occurrences that had already taken place during the year. Just before she pressed the power button, she could hear one of the newscasters say, "2019 has been a year full of surprises."

The day ahead promised to be eventful, which also meant that Desirae couldn't stomach a large breakfast. She instead prepared and sat with a small cup of espresso from the stainless espresso maker placed in the center of the marble countertop.

After a few minutes, she grabbed a banana from a gold-plated fruit bowl in the center of the table and tossed her keys and cell phone into her purse before heading out to the garage. She was lucky enough to have left in time to beat the hectic morning rush hour traffic that plagued downtown Atlanta.

Arriving at her destination, Desirae pulled into the parking lot and stepped out of the car, a sight to behold.

She stood 5'6, with a dark complexion, a blunt-cut bob that dropped to right above her shoulders, and an hourglass shape. She walked across the parking lot into the building bristling with confidence. The elevator doors slid open at her approach, seemingly anticipating her arrival. She gently glided her fingers along her hair to make sure it was in place, shifted her skirt slightly, and stood up tall before exiting.

As she walked toward her office, a familiar voice began speaking just behind her. "These are the hard copies for the meeting."

"Thank you, Samantha," said Desiree as she accepted the folder and began to peruse the papers inside before turning and asking, "Have you heard from the Smiths?"

"Not yet, but I will place a follow-up call this morning."

"Thank you. If we need to schedule lunch or anything, go ahead. I'm thinking a face-to-face meeting might make the difference that we need."

"Okay, I'll do that. Also, Mr. Thomas called to confirm brunch for Friday."

Desirae pressed her lips together while raising an eyebrow. "Hmm. That should still work for my schedule."

"Okay, perfect. Here's your coffee." Samantha extended the cup toward Desirae.

They both looked toward the boardroom door when one of the partners of the firm passed by, heading to the same conference room where they were meeting.

Samantha noticed that Desirae needed confirmation. "You have this in the bag. We are claiming it now."

Desirae smiled, took a sip of the coffee, and gently set the mug back on the desk before walking into the conference room.

Jennifer

"Please say yes. Please say yes. Please say yes." A faint voice could be heard from the confines of the bathroom in the early evening hours. The darkness of the night was revealed just behind the curtains as the wind blew in fresh air through the open bedroom window.

Jennifer was hovering over the bathroom counter, one hand holding up her weight and the other clutching a pregnancy test. With closed eyes, she repeated, "Please say yes" once more.

The faint beep of the test signaling its completion prompted her to open her eyes. She bit her bottom lip in dismay and threw the test across the bathroom. With tears streaming down her face, she stumbled backward until her back was pressed against the wall. She began to cry as she slid to the floor in defeat.

With her face pressed into her hand, she yelled out in rage, "What is wrong with me? I'm broken."

She lay in a fetal position on the floor, crying until a voice spoke, reminding her of the life she had forgotten at the moment.

"Babe, you almost ready?"

Jennifer jumped up, wiping her face hastily before responding, "Yes, bae. Just a few more minutes."

After peeling herself from the floor completely, Jennifer held on to the corner of the counter to stand up and proceeded to splash her face with cold water. She looked into the mirror and smiled, as if to give herself grace. Kneeling down to retrieve a hand towel from a basket under the sink, she heard the crinkling of a plastic bag. Carefully pulling it to the front of the cabinet, she peered in at the countless failed tests she had taken before. She scrambled to retrieve the most recent test, which had landed across the bathroom amidst her frustration, and added it to the count. Another deep sigh allowed her to exhale the pain that her unanswered prayers had caused.

She attempted once more to smile through the pain as she placed the bag back under the counter and pushed it to the back so that it was hidden amidst the toiletries. Grabbing the towel, she dried her face, mumbling, "Pull yourself together. You've got a husband who loves you and the life you've always dreamed of. Get it together."

Reaching for the tube of pink lipstick on the counter and applying it seemed to bring her back to focus. She ran her fingers through her hair and exhaled again before spraying a bit of perfume and walking to the door.

As she went into the foyer with her head down, she heard a voice say, "You look beautiful."

The sentiment caused her to lift her head and say, "Thank you, baby. I thought you weren't going to make it tonight."

Derek replied with a look of exhaustion, "I caught hell, but I was able to get out of there. I know we need this night. I couldn't mess it up." He reached to kiss Jennifer while grabbing a handful of her ass. Jennifer playfully pushed him away, knowing if it was up to Derek they would stay in for sex.

Hand in hand, Derek and Jennifer exited the front door and went to their garage. Derek sped up his pace to beat Jennifer to the passenger's side of the car and lifted the handle, extending one arm to help her in. Jennifer slid into the car, and Derek closed the door behind her. He walked to the driver's side and got into the car, placing the keys in the ignition. He looked into Jennifer's eyes and smiled. After the exchange, she turned toward the front window and sank into the seat, giving him a broad smile.

Driving down Buckhead Avenue, Jennifer peered out of the window with a look of despair. Derek noticed and asked, "What's wrong?"

"Nothing, I'm just a little tired. It's been a long day."

Derek reached over and grabbed Jennifer's hand, pulling it toward his face and gently kissing the back of it.

Recognizing his effort, Jennifer responded, "Thank you for all you do. I don't know what I would do without you."

Derek laughed. "You don't have to figure out where you would be, because we will always be together."

Their eyes met briefly, and they laughed in unison until the radio caught Derek's attention. He dropped Jennifer's hand and turned the volume up. "Come on, don't play like this ain't our song!"

He bounced his shoulders to the beat, becoming more animated until Jennifer caught his mood. Hesitant at first, she finally found herself dancing and singing along and receiving even more pleasure from the moment than Derek.

She danced without care or worry until they reached the restaurant. When they pulled up, the valet was standing at Derek's side to escort him out of the car. He walked around to Jennifer's side and waited to reach for her hand until after the valet assisted her. The hostess opened the restaurant door and smiled to welcome them in. They walked up the brick steps to the threshold. Upon entrance, they stopped at the hostess' table.

"Good evening. Do you have a reservation?"

"Yes. It should be under Derek McKinley."

"Great. It will be just a few minutes for us to have you seated. We are clearing a table for you now."

"Thank you."

"Is there a special occasion tonight?"

"Every night and every day with this beautiful lady is a special occasion."

"Aww. Yes, sir. Indeed."

Jennifer looked over at Derek, smiling as he wrapped his arm around her waist and pulled her close to him. They both exhaled in each other's grasp until the hostess notified them that it was time to be seated.

She led them through the restaurant to a quaint table facing a large glass window. Derek pulled out Jennifer's chair and gently slid her up to the table.

After Derek took his own seat, the waitress approached. "Good evening, I'll be serving you tonight. May I start by getting you something to drink?"

Derek took the liberty to order for both of them. "Yes, two glasses of chardonnay ..."

Jennifer interrupted, "No, water for me, please." After nodding her head to confirm with the waitress, Jennifer glared at Derek.

Feeling guilty, he looked at Jennifer and back at the waitress before changing his selection. "I'm so sorry. Yes, two glasses of water, please."

The waitress hesitantly confirmed, "I'll be right back with two glasses of water. Please take your time in reviewing our menu and let me know if you have any questions that I can be of assistance with."

"Thank you," Jennifer replied.

When the hostess left, Derek reached across the table to request Jennifer's hands, but she turned her head in an attempt to ignore his gesture. "Bae. Look at me." Reluctantly, she made eye contact. "It slipped my mind. I know you've been working hard to follow the instructions from Dr. Taylor, and I should be more sensitive to it. I'm sorry."

Jennifer let out a sigh and placed her hand within Derek's, still open to receive hers. "It's okay. I know you have a lot on your plate and probably forgot."

They smiled at each other and sat back in their respective chairs, regaining some sense of normalcy from the moment.

"How was work?"

"It was good. Robert is still going on and on about his new idea for a business."

"Are you considering it?"

"I don't know. Like I was telling him, it's not a simple decision to just go full throttle with the business and have no plan B. I have a wife, and we're trying to expand our family. I can't just quit my job and start a new company."

"Yes, but you're too talented to limit yourself. We're a team, so we'll get through whatever comes with you starting a new company. We got this."

Derek's phone rang, and he nodded and smiled at Jennifer to excuse himself from the table. He walked toward the extended corridor outside of the restrooms, whispering, "Hey."

The voice on the other end inquired, "Hey. Are you busy?"

"I'm at dinner with Jenn, but I have a minute."

"I missed you."

"You just ain't know how much I missed you."

"If that was true, I would've been heard from you."

"I can't argue with that. I've had a lot going on lately, but I'll hopefully see you soon."

"Don't play games with me, Derek."

"Rebecca, believe me, I'm not. I'm still remembering that dress."

"What about it?"

Derek bit his bottom lip and said, "I liked everything about it. The way it hugged your hips. It had me thinking about the last time I saw you without it and what I did to you." Lost in a trance, Derek got entangled in the conversation. A random passerby headed into the men's restroom brought him back to reality.

"I have to go. I'll call you back later."

"Okay."

Derek hung up and walked back to the table with Jennifer.

"Everything okay?" she inquired.

He shrugged. "Yes, work stuff."

Jennifer looked at Derek with annoyance as he picked up where they'd left off.

"But I was thinking we should switch things up this year for our anniversary."

"Like what?"

"I don't know exactly where, but let's get away. Things have been too stressful lately."

Smiling at his thoughtfulness, Jennifer responded with excitement. "Okay, I like the idea."

"You pick the place and just let me know."

"Sounds like a plan! What's my budget?"

"Don't ask that crazy question. It's whatever you want."

Derek slid his seat around to Jennifer's side of the table and put his arm around her. They enjoyed the rest of the evening at the table in each other's arms before retreating home to end the night cuddled tightly in bed.

Ashlee

The large stainless steel hood installed over the shiny black stovetop with eight eyes and a custom griddle was a chef's dream. The sea of marble on the countertops and the floors served as perfect accessories to the Italian cherry wood cabinets, some as tall as six feet bearing crown molding. The stainless steel appliances operated by voice and expansive revolving pantry and built-in chef's quarters were indicators that the kitchen belonged to a house of privilege.

Just behind the oversized island, Ashlee could be seen chopping and grating, stirring and beating a host of ingredients. Her level of intensity was apparent from the moments in which she stood on her toes while pressing her hand firmly on top of the knife to dice the vegetables. She meant business and had every intention of completing the task at hand. She heard a familiar voice just as she turned around to retrieve a bag of brown sugar from the pantry.

"You need help?"

Allowing him to laugh at her expense, she slid out of the way, making room for the man to step forward and easily reach the can on the shelf that hadn't been as easily attainable for her.

"Will, it's not funny. You know I'm short," Ashlee proclaimed.

Will handed Ashlee the brown sugar with a smirk. "What does that have to do with me?"

"I think you purposely put things on that top shelf so that you can laugh at me."

Leaning onto the countertop, Will demonstrated that he was further vested in the exchange.

While rolling her eyes, Ashlee poured a portion of brown sugar into a sauté pan with honey and butter.

Will leaned in and teased, "If you say so! What's on the menu tonight, Chef Ashlee?"

"Salmon, wild rice pilaf, and white chocolate-strawberry tiramisu for dessert."

Bewildered, Will replied, "What is wild rice pilaf?"

Ashlee jokingly replied, "I'm not telling you because then you are not going to want to eat it."

"Oh, so I suppose you just know everything?"

"I know you, and I know food. You, sir, have to be surprised. The truth is your palette is worse than a five-year-old's."

"Mannn, whatever."

Will reached for a bowl of rice that he assumed was the wild rice pilaf in an attempt to taste it prematurely. Ashlee tapped his hand with her wooden spoon. "What part of you have to wait don't you understand?" she mocked.

Will laughed. "My God, you are so mean."

"I'm going to start treating you like my son in a minute."

"Yeah. Yeah. Yeah. How is the little man?"

Her face was instantly illuminated before she replied, "He's great. Getting bigger by the day with plenty of energy."

"I'm telling you, you need to go ahead and put a ball in his hand. Start him early."

"Absolutely not!"

"Why not? The earlier the better. Give him a chance to get comfortable with it."

"No. I don't want him getting hurt, and I don't want him to think sports is the only way to succeed in life."

"That has nothing to do with starting football early."

"To me it does. If he wants to play when he gets older, I won't stop him. But for now, it's a no go."

Will walked to the fridge to get a bottle of water out and took a sip before speaking again. "How does Zavier feel about it?"

"Of course, like most men, he wants him to play. But he respects my feelings on it and agreed to wait a little longer."

"He's a good one. I would've snuck him on a field and warned him not to tell his momma."

"And we would be fighting."

Will started to imitate boxing moves in the air. "Duck and weave. Duck and weave," he said jokingly.

"Ugh, you get on my nerves."

Ashlee rolled her eyes at Will's annoyance. "So who's showing up tonight?"

"What are you talking about?"

"Which one of your little groupies showing up tonight?"

Will pretended to not know what Ashlee was talking about before remembering that she knew better. He dropped his head, muttering, "Nadia."

"I can't keep up with you."

"Don't do that. This one is special."

"Sure. I'll bet she is special until her time is up and the next one comes along."

Leaning his back against the oversized refrigerator, Will looked Ashlee in the eyes and said, "No, she's different." At her dubious expression, he insisted, "You'll see when she gets here. For the first time in my life, I feel like my heart is good with her."

Eyebrows raised, Ashlee replied, "Wow. I mean wow. I've never heard you say anything close to that."

"The truth is, I've never met anyone like her. And even though she hasn't been in my life for long, when you know you just know."

"Well, I look forward to meeting the new love of your life."

Smirking, Will replied, "In due time, Ash. In due time."

CHAPTER 2

SCATTERED

Needing a quick break from the office and an outfit for Miami, Desirae found herself in Phipps Plaza doing some quick shopping with her friend Brian. Anxious to see Malik, she wanted to ensure she got an outfit that would leave him speechless and that his money was well spent.

With hands raised, and shoulders lifted, he asked, "Why did you drag me to this mall like I don't have work to be doing?"

"Don't act like that. You love spending time with me. Plus, I need you to help me find something to wear for Miami."

Puzzled by her response, Brian asked, "Umm, what's in Miami? What am I missing?"

With a sneaky smirk, Desirae whispered, "Malik."

"Why are you smiling like that when you say his name?"

"Because I know you're going to have something to say."

At the perfect moment, the two came across an upscale boutique that was nestled in the corner.

"Let's stop in here," Desirae said, excited by the potential options.

Once inside, they noticed all of the mannequins dressed in upscale dresses with the designer price tags to match. Brian grabbed Desirae's hand and led her to one rack in particular, flanked by pastel colors. Intrigued with all the options, they began to sort through each rack to determine what was worthy of trying on. The options quickly stacked up on Brian's arm while they continued their conversation. After snagging a red dress from the rack behind them, Desirae held it up for Brian's approval before inquiring, "So you have nothing to say?"

Brian pressed his lips together and looked the other way, shaking his head in disapproval. "You already know how I feel. I'm all for having fun and everything. Shit, you single with no kids, live your life. But play by the rules."

"Here you go with the damn rules."

"You say that, but you've yet to move differently. I don't like how you're always readily available when he wants to see you." In the heat of the moment, he took a step back and placed his hand up to pause before continuing, "He needs to think that you're busy and he's a second thought to you. But your ass is raising your hand on some *pick me, pick me* when he wants to come around."

Desirae smiled and then laughed like a schoolgirl talking about her first crush. "You are being so extra right now. I do not act like that."

"Yes, you do. Then I have to hear you complain when his rude ass ghosts you."

Unable to rebut Brian's claims, Desirae remained silent. "Exactly, I need you to treat him the same way you treat these other men. It's like you lose all your standards for him, and it's not a good look."

"I get what you're saying, but I don't feel the need to make Malik jump through those hoops when I know what it is and neither of us wants anything serious." Desirae sighed as she pulled a dress from the rack, holding their choices and going into the nearby dressing room.

"This right here is a perfect example. Why are you buying something for Miami and not him? He should be doing way more for you."

"For one, he is funding this purchase. Secondly, I'm not about to be one of those girls walking around waiting for a man to do for me. I'm not built that way. I work hard, so if I want something, I can get it without any stipulations."

"Well, you should have started with he's paying."

Brian went and pulled a dress off a different rack, sliding it through the dressing room curtain.

Desirae read the tag and gasped, "3000?!"

"You said he was paying, so try it on! Furthermore, what about David?"

"What about him?"

"Where does he fit in? I thought you liked him."

Desirae spun around once and glanced at herself in the mirror before walking about the dressing room to showcase the dress he'd picked. "I do like him. He's a sweetheart."

Mid conversation, she retreated back to the dressing room as Brian rolled his eyes. He wrapped his arm around the curtain, suggesting another dress for Desirae to try before continuing, "Well, if that's the case, then why are you still dealing with Malik so heavy?"

Desirae reentered the dressing room. "I like David, I do!"

"It sounds like you trying to convince yourself that you like him, not me."

"Moment of transparency?"

"Yes, always."

"He is everything I thought I wanted, but for some reason, I don't feel any sparks. Not the kind that makes me want to be committed to only him."

"Well, honey, if it's not there then it's not there. I have an idea, and I want you to be open-minded."

Desirae exited the dressing room. "What?"

"Wow! That dress is everything on you!" Brian paused. "It's the cinched waist for me. It's the fact that it's black for me. Honey, it's giving bandage dress realness and I'm here for it." Waving his hand in the air with excitement, he continued, "Let me set you up on a blind date."

"Not!" Desirae shook her head as if Brian's mission was impossible.

"You're going on the date. I know what you like. See, you need a good blend of David and Malik, and I'm going to find it."

"Fine! But if I don't like him, I'm not sitting through a whole date." Desirae departed the dressing room, and the two headed toward the register to make the purchase.

"I'll be your escape plan if you need it. Just text me, and I'll call like it's an emergency."

The cashier placed Desirae's dress into a bag. "Your total is $2100 today."

"Sheesh!"

Brian quickly reassured her, "Don't stress over it. If he sent you the money, spend it all."

"Ugh!" Desirae grunted as she reluctantly handed over her card.

"But back to this blind date. What three things do you know you want the guy to have?"

"A good job, no kids, and a nice physique. That's minimum."

"Okay, that's still manageable."

"I think so. I mean, why wouldn't it be?"

"All I know is that deep down inside, you want, need, and deserve better. And when you get back from this weekend rendezvous with Malik, we're going to find what you are looking for." Desirae nodded as if she still needed to be convinced that it was possible.

"And I know you have to finish getting the rest of the things on your list for the trip. I just couldn't let you do the dress shopping on your own. Honey, you needed me on that one!"

"And you're right about that. I need you period. Thanks for being a friend."

"Anytime, girl. Anytime."

After saying their goodbyes, Desirae finished off her list and patiently waited for her weekend of escapades to begin.

Let's Misbehave

The sound of Jhene Aiko piped through the walls, roaring from the living room into the bedroom in the early hours of the morning. Semi darkness fought to peer in from the windows. Jennifer could be seen nestled under the covers and breathing heavily, deep in slumber, until the music interrupted her. She sat up slowly in bed, squinting to make sense of it all. As her vision came into focus, she zeroed in on Derek, shirtless and covered only by his red and green plaid pajama pants. The drawstring dangled just over his man parts, and Jennifer was instantly aroused.

As he got closer to the bed, he began to speak. "I thought I'd wake you up with your favorite music. You know, to set the mood."

"Set the mood? Mood for what?" Jennifer questioned with a smile on her face.

Derek shrugged his shoulders. "The mood for our anniversary vacation. We leave in a few days, you know."

"Of course I know. I can't wait."

"The truth is, I'm the luckiest man in the world because of you."

Jennifer wrapped her arms around his neck and said, "You are my heart, Derek. And no matter what happens, I will always be by your side. For better or worse."

"Aight, aight, woman. We ain't having no bad times." Their burst of united laughter filled the room until their bellies hurt. They were lost in bliss until an untimely text notification caused Derek's phone to vibrate on the nightstand.

He reached to power his phone off so they wouldn't be interpreted. Before doing so, he noticed the text read, *I woke up with you on my mind. I have to see you.*

Startled by Jennifer's inquiry of "Who is that?" he gently slammed the phone down while holding the power button until it was no longer illuminated.

"Nobody. Whatever it was, it will have to wait until I get into the office. Nothing is more important than you right now." They remained in each other's embrace, exchanging intimate kisses for what felt like an eternity.

As the daylight broke through the bedroom windows, Derek recognized that time was now of the essence. "You stay right here and enjoy this music before you begin your day. I've got to get up and get ready. Mondays are always crazy at the office."

Jennifer pushed Derek back against the headboard, leaving him in a sitting position. She made her way down to his pelvis, taking slow breaks to kiss certain spots of his stomach. Looking up at him, she said, "Well, I'm not letting you go anywhere until you give me a piece of you."

"Oh, that's how you feel? We might make a baby this morning."

Although Jennifer felt uneasy about Derek's comment, she didn't allow it to ruin the mood. After all, he had no idea of everything Jennifer had been through to conceive.

Jennifer slid off Derek's bottoms with the help of him lifting his hips. She started at the bottom of his dick with her tongue slowly gliding upward as if it was a lollipop, all while looking him in the eyes. Once she made it to the head, she immediately consumed all of him, taking in as much of his dick as she could. She sucked and slurped in a rotating motion while massaging his dick with her tongue. She could feel the saliva collecting in her mouth as she slid his dick in and out and made a swallowing gesture when it was fully positioned in her mouth, driving Derek crazy.

"Babe, damn," Derek said while rubbing her shoulders and arms before settling back into his starting position. Derek's response to her actions only further stimulated Jennifer. She loved to see him enjoying her.

She let off from sucking and readjusted her body, but not before giving an intense suck of the head. Now lying flat with her face resting next to his hip and one hand jerking his dick, Jennifer sucked one of his balls into her mouth. She gently massaged it with her tongue, being careful not to apply too much force. When she noticed him getting comfortable, she began rotating between each ball while keeping a good rhythm stroking his dick. The next time she moved to switch, she slid her tongue a little more south, first resting on his gooch but then finding her way to his ass. She nailed her mark by the way Derek pulled a pillow over his face and squirmed his pelvis around. She began to flicker her tongue around his backdoor entrance. Between the up and down circular motions of her hand and the spit squashed around with her tongue wetting his ass, it wasn't long before Jennifer was engulfing Derek's dick in time to feel it pulsating in her mouth as semen shot to the back of her throat. Once it was clear that he was empty, she took one solid swallow, sat up, and looked at him with a smirk on her face.

Diced Pineapples

By the time Desirae arrived at the airport the next morning, she realized that even after a full night's sleep, she was still tired. Although she hadn't disclosed it to anyone, work was taking more of a toll on her than she let on. The plane ride would be her only chance to get some rest before her weekend tryst with Malik.

The only way that Desirae knew they had landed in Miami was by the announcement made by the attendant. After deplaning, she stopped at the gate to ask one of the staff members for directions to baggage claim.

Upon her arrival there, she noticed a sizable man dressed in a black suit, holding a sign bearing her name. Near his feet, she recognized that he had already retrieved her luggage.

When she got within conversational distance of him, he began to speak. "Ms. Sanders, I am your driver for your stay here in Miami." And before she knew it, she found herself in the back seat of an extended black luxury town car being whisked away to the hotel that Malik had reserved.

When they arrived, a neon sign on the front of the tall white building that read Hotel B.Allure. The driver came around to open her door, offered his hand to assist her out, collected her belongings, and escorted her to the desk to check in.

"Wait here," he said after entering the lobby. Desirae took a seat on the plush purple couch next to the fragrant row of flowers and looked around. Shortly thereafter, the driver returned to her. "Everything was arranged by Mr. Mallard before your arrival. Here is your room key. You will be staying on the 32nd floor. I have arranged for your bags to be delivered if you'd like to go up now."

Although he was suggesting, it was obvious to Desirae that he was also encouraging her to go. The driver nodded gently and exited through the same doors where they'd entered. Desirae stood up and looked around. The substantial lobby made her feel small. It was luxuriously appointed as if they had been commanded to create a fusion of Roman history and art deco. The tall gold columns were a sight to behold. As she began walking toward the elevators, the bright hues consisting of pink and turquoise seemed to jump out amidst the white marble floors. The rays of the sun were relentless and only second in her attention span to the buzz of the lobby.

Within ten minutes of being in the lobby, she had sighted at least three celebrities, which reminded her that she was officially in Miami. She smiled to herself as her mind transitioned from work to vacation mode. By the time she reached the elevator doors, she was ready, willing, and able for whatever Malik had in mind.

The ride up to the room in the glass elevator allowed her to appreciate the beauty of South Beach. She could see not only inside of the hotel lobby but also the ocean in the distance. It was a beautiful reminder to not allow the perils of work to consume her. She used her reflection in the glass to tidy her hair. She wanted to look perfect for Malik. When she exited the elevator, she discovered that the room was just to the left. Standing outside of the door, she paused to stand a little taller and adjust her boobs. Inserting the key with anticipation, she opened the door and walked in with an enormous smile on her face. There was a sense of stillness that led her to announce, "Malik. I made it."

A glance around made it clear that Malik had spared no expense for the room. It was indeed a penthouse suite, which likely explained why he hadn't heard her enter. "Malik," she said once more, now exploring the individual rooms until reaching the master bedroom. She was led to a note on the bed that read, "Hey beautiful. I had to step away for business, but I will be back soon. Please make yourself comfortable." Slightly disappointed, but accepting, she ventured over to the oversized windows that extended from floor to ceiling. One window, in particular, gave way to a handle that opened to a terrace overlooking the water.

Entranced by the ambiance, she closed her eyes and soaked up the sound of the waves, lost in bliss until the sound of her phone interrupted the moment.

A text from Jennifer checking in to see if she had arrived safely was a gentle reminder that she was loved. Although she hadn't noticed it previously, a Tiffany blue silk dress was draped across the bed. She knew instantly that Malik had purchased it for her to wear that night. She immediately took off her clothes and slipped the dress over her head to try it on. After seeing herself in the mirror, she decided to remove her bra, allowing the material to drape lower over her breast. As she turned around in the mirror, she admired the curvature of her hips and the way the dress stopped just below her knees. When she was done playing dress-up, she decided to shower before Malik arrived back in the room.

The bathroom was appointed with an abundance of amenities, which led her to stay in longer than she expected. Lost in the moment, she belted out Keyshia Cole as if she was performing for a sold-out audience. Standing in the shower, she found peace and allowed herself to bask in it. When Desirae exited the shower, she grabbed an over-sized bath towel from the towel warmer in the bathroom and dried off while walking back toward the bedroom.

She was startled to see Malik sitting on the bed. She hadn't heard him enter. "Malik! Damn. You scared the shit out of me."

"I should say the same thing," he replied sarcastically. "Is that how you greet me after not having seen me for a min-ute? Come on girl, you know what I want."

Desirae allowed the towel to drop to the floor as she stared at Malik. Watching him examine every inch of her body with his eyes was turning her on even more. She stepped directly in front of him and began to touch her-self, slowly sliding her fingers across her full breasts, to her small waist, settling in between her thighs. Malik, notice-ably aroused, leaned back, making his hard dick create a tent in his pants. Desirae continued to touch herself, now sliding her fingers in and out of her pussy, with each fin-ger becoming wetter and wetter from her juices. As Malik noticed Desirae reaching the point of no return, he inter-rupted her by instructing her to taste her fingers.

She smirked and lifted her finger to her mouth, first lick-ing it as if it were a lollipop and then sliding it into her mouth.

Malik nodded for her to come to him. She reached for his pants to undo his belt buckle and motioned for him to lift the lower half of his body so that she could remove his jeans and underwear. Her only goal at the moment was to mount him, and she did, settling at his pelvis. He slid his arms under her thighs and forcefully pulled her body up to his face. Locked into the moment, she felt his tongue gliding against her pussy in an upward motion toward her clitoris. She was weakening by the second.

Malik, clearly in his element, indulged in her sweetness. She gripped his arms and closed her eyes as she drifted away in pleasure. Witnessing her coming close to satisfaction, Malik turned his attention to her clitoris, generously shifting between sucking and slow circular movements with his tongue. Desiree moaned and thrust against his face, furthering Malik's arousal. His dick was now fully hardened and awaiting the opportunity for penetration.

As Desiree got closer to climaxing, Malik slid his hands to her ass, grasping every ounce of her soft round curves his hands could hold while intensifying the strokes of his tongue. He slipped one of his fingers into her ass while continuing to suck on her pussy. Although Malik was present at the moment, Desirae was overtaken by an intense tingling sensation signifying that her soul had left her body. If Malik was unsure whether his job was accomplished, the way she lay motionless next to him was all the evidence he needed.

The plans to go out turned into a night in with room service. The next day was a blur with lust for breakfast and passion for lunch. By the time dinner rolled around, they were both too tired from their Olympic conquests to leave the room. Instead, they found themselves talking at 3:00 a.m. They were both starving, so Malik called in a favor to the driver that had escorted Desirae to the hotel to bring them hamburgers and french fries from Checkers, the only thing that was open in the city at that hour. They devoured the food in bed and laughed as if they were old friends. The next morning, they fell asleep once again, this time as the sun rose on the horizon and Desirae held on as tightly to Malik as she could, reckoning that in a few short hours, she would be back on a plane heading to her own bed.

Desirae always enjoyed her time with Malik because it carried no expectations, allowing her to live within her comfort zone of running from vulnerability and commitment. His career as a sports agent lent itself to many exploits and conquests, so they mastered living in the moment when time allowed. She understood that Malik's interest did not reach much beyond her physicality, and spending too much time with him would only cause her pain eventually, but the short moments they shared seemed to be the perfect antidote for her.

Family Affair

Ashlee pulled up to her house and noticed that the lights were still on. Exhausted from a long day of work, she took the time to relax before entering the surge of energy that she knew awaited her inside. Making the most of the momentary downtime, she began to go through missed emails and text messages, responding accordingly. Just as she was reaching the end, a FaceTime call came in with the name Janay.

"Hey, bae. What are you doing?"

Ashlee gave a gentle smirk and responded, "Just pulled up to the house. Going through messages before I head inside. It was a long night. Will invited more people than I was expecting. About eight extra people showed up which threw everything off."

In disbelief, Janay replied, "Well, I hope you spoke up and addressed it. If you didn't say anything, he's going to keep doing it. Furthermore, you have a son to think of. You can't spend so much time there."

Irritated by Janay's unwanted opinion, Ashlee sat in silence before responding. "I'm not saying that you're wrong, but Will is one of my better-paying clients. I can't fuck this up because he's annoying at times. He knows a lot of people."

Janay felt the tension and responded with a softer tone, "It's your career, so do as you please, just don't lose sight of what's important. I've seen it happen too many times to other people."

Ashlee rolled her eyes and let out a deep sigh. "It's been a long day, and the last thing I'm trying to deal with is the negativity." The two said their goodbyes and ended the call.

Ashlee grasped for as much energy as she could before grabbing her belongings and entering the house. She walked through the front door and immediately tripped over Nolan's toys that were splattered out across the floor. The noise of her tripping caught Nolan's attention, and he ran to embrace his mom by jumping in her arms.

Noticing Xavier sitting on the sofa, she asked Nolan, "Why are you still up?"

He excitedly responded, "Daddy said I could stay up and wait on you." Nolan jumped down and returned to his toys, which had taken over the living room floor as well. Ashlee dropped her belongings on the kitchen table and flopped down on the sofa, stretching her legs out across his lap.

Without breaking eye contact from the football game on the television, Xavier asked, "Long night, I'm assuming?"

Ashlee dropped her head back and firmly replied, "Yes, and I don't want to talk about it."

Nolan broke from playing with his toys to ask his mom if his dad was going to spend the night, implying that Xavier would cook pancakes in the morning. Ashlee looked at Xavier, who at this point could feel her glaring at him from his peripheral vision.

"You told him you were staying?" Ashlee asked.

Xavier laughed and responded, "Yeah, he wouldn't stop asking me to."

"I swear you let him just do whatever. You over there laughing; furthermore, how will Vicky feel about you staying here?"

Realizing that Nolan was still functioning at full speed, Ashlee interrupted the conversation to instruct Nolan to go clean his room so that his dad could read him a story before bed. Excited that both his parents would be with him tonight, Nolan sped off to his bedroom to transform the mess that awaited.

"She'll be all right," Xavier stated, shrugging his shoulder.

"You say that now, but we both know that she is going to trip when she finds out you stayed over here. You know our style of co-parenting can be uncomfortable for other people. Yet you go find the most controlling and insecure woman ever," Ashlee insisted.

Xavier quickly rebutted, "Well, the way I look at it, what we got is already established and Lil' Man is happy. I'm not adjusting this for anyone. They are going to have to accept it or be gone."

"You say that now, but then I have to deal with you complaining about the nagging."

Xavier cut off the television and stood to stretch. "Does it matter? You like being in my business anyways," he said, giving Ashlee a smirk.

"Whatever! Can you go check on your son? You know it takes him two seconds to get distracted," Ashlee affirmed.

Xavier laughed and left the room to go help Nolan get ready for bed.

Soul Food

Perched on a bench with a view overlooking the city, Jennifer soaked up the rays of the sharp Atlanta sun. She allowed herself to feel the warmth on her face before smiling to herself and dropping her head gently while caressing her stomach. It was almost as if she was in a secret conversation with her womb and the universe, hopeful, praying for new life to make her whole until reality set in. Her smile faded at the sound of cooing and the sight of another woman pushing a baby in a stroller. Jennifer wondered if she would ever be worthy enough to earn the coveted title of *mother*.

In a desperate attempt to remove her mind from the sea of sadness, she unfolded her legs, allowing her bare feet to touch the grass as she reached down to remove her laptop from her Louis Vuitton bucket bag. Somehow feeling unworthy inspired her to write about self-love. The words flowed from her fingertips effortlessly. And for a moment, she was lost in the whirlwind of her words and emotions.

Unbeknownst to Derek, Jennifer had long maintained a women's empowerment blog, cultivating a sizable following over time. Although Derek had never mentioned it, she had managed over time to configure her idea of what she believed the perfect wife to be. The prospect of anything outside of that idea scared her. Perfect wives weren't writers; they didn't maintain blogs that empowered women to be themselves. Perfect wives knew when to speak and when to tame their tongues. They didn't cause commotions and rally the troupes; instead, they focused their attention on pleasing their husbands and maintaining peace, or so she thought. The thoughts in her head and the desires of her heart didn't always align, which is why she often found herself committing her words to paper in silence and secret.

As she prepared to write the last paragraph, she was interrupted by the vibration of her phone. A voice on the other end began speaking before she could utter the word hello.

"So how's the blog coming? Have you told Derrick about it yet? Maybe the sooner he finds out, you can both move forward to make me an abuela."

Jennifer listened intently while rolling her eyes in the back of her head. "Mom, you know I can't tell him about this blog yet. He's already pressuring me to quit my current job."

"Well, you're going to have to tell him sometime. Besides, I've never seen anything make you happier than when you write and pour your heart out onto the pages. And speaking of happiness, it would be nice to have some little nietos running around. I could keep the kids while you and Derek work each day. It would do my heart good to have some new additions to the family. We haven't had babies in almost a decade now."

Jennifer dropped her head in shame while listening to her mother's words. Only she knew how difficult her journey to motherhood had been.

"Yeah, Mom. I hear you loud and clear today, just like I do every day when we talk, and you remind me that you want me to give you grandkids. I'm starting to feel like you're not even worried about me anymore, just the grandkids on the way."

"Hija, you know better than that. I will always be there for you," her mother confirmed.

"You always on that phone," a startling voice stated.

"Hey girl, Mamacita, let me call you back. Desirae just got here, and we desperately need to catch up!"

"Okay, hija. Give the girls my love."

"Okay, I will. Love you."

"Love you more," her mother said as she hung up the phone.

Jennifer turned toward Desirae with excitement. Desirae, always slightly overdressed, wore a tight black pencil skirt, pink silk burgundy mock neck bodysuit, Tom Ford heels, Chanel black/gold belt, and an oversized Prada bag. Her Versace frames were big enough to block the sun and expression from her eyes, but Jennifer knew there was a warm smile and an even warmer heart underneath it all.

Desirae plopped down onto the bench and wrapped her arm through Jennifer's. "Girl, I never really admit this out loud, so if you tell someone I said it, I'll never actually admit it, but work is kicking my ass." Jennifer turned toward her attentively. "I mean, making partner sounds good in theory, but I'm not sure if it's really what I want anymore," Jennifer added.

"Sis, you are talking crazy right now. I know that you're exhausted. Hell, you're carrying a lot on your shoulders, but you have not come this far to only come this far. Do you hear me?"

Desirae lit up from Jennifer's words of encouragement. "See this is why I need my girls. I mean it's hard enough trying to navigate this thing called life, not to mention love."

"You can say that again," Jennifer concurred.

"And speaking of love, how is my brother Derek treating you?"

Jennifer looked down but snapped her head back up quickly, revealing a hint of a smile. "Girl, Derek is Derek. You know he treats me like a Queen. I couldn't complain about that man if I tried."

"You got a good one," Desirae interjected.

"Now he's not perfect, but I do think he's perfect for me," Jennifer gushed.

"I'd have to agree with you there. You did good, girl." They exchanged high fives and snapped their fingers in agreement with one another. Amidst their cheering, a voice could be heard in the distance.

"What's up, Queens? I know I'm late, but I made it." Ashlee walked over and collapsed in a nearby chair.

"I was wondering if you were still coming. I know you've had some long nights working for the new client," Jennifer said.

"What's his name again?" Desirae inquired.

"Oh. I think you're speaking of Will. I do work late hours when cooking for Will and his infamous dinner parties. It's cool, though. He's pretty dope."

"That's good, but don't let him run you ragged, honey. You have to balance work and Nolan," Desirae cautioned.

"You can say that again," Jennifer agreed.

"Y'all are right, it's just that my career is picking up right now and it feels good," says Ashlee. "I can say that working for Will is one of the first times that I didn't feel like I had to hide who I was, which is kind of cool."

"That's what's up," Desirae interjected.

"While you're over there all on her case, make sure you find a balance too," Jennifer reminded them.

"I will admit, work has taken a toll on me. It's like I'm expected to show up, to look a certain way, act a certain way, and smile pretty, and pretend that everything is okay. Meanwhile, no one is saying a word when the male partners leave at 5 for drinks with the boys while I'm stuck in the office working. At times, it feels like it's a man's world," Desirae proclaimed.

"I'm just sick of society, that's the game wherever you go... if you chose to play by the rules," Ashlee shrieked.

Jennifer lifted her hand as if she were giving praise in a church choir. "Yesss! My mother once told me that if I could overcome my fear of darkness, then I would never have to be afraid of anything else in my life." Ashlee and Desirae both had puzzled looks on their faces. Jennifer continued,

"What she meant was that if I could be okay by myself, then the rest of my life would fall into place."

"I get it. After my marriage to Xavier didn't work, my saving grace was letting go of the labels and the need to be accepted by anyone other than myself, and my son of course," Desirae interjected.

"That's the most real thing I've heard all day. I don't think the world acknowledges how much pressure we face as women. And let's not even talk about the burden of being women of color."

"Girl, we don't have enough time in the day to go there," said Ashlee.

"So listen, I know that everyone is busy, but I think we should get together for dinner at the top of next week before I leave for Turks and Caicos with Derek," Jennifer said. "I mean really, both of you will have major updates, and I need all the tea!"

"All right, how about Monday night?" Desirae suggested.

"Works for me as long as it's before 6. I've got to be at Will's house to prep at 8."

"It's a date. And I'm sending a calendar invite now to both of you, so you don't forget," Jennifer persisted.

"Okay, I have to get out of here to take Nolan to Andretti's before I go back to work tonight," Ashlee said.

"Me too. I need to finish packing for tomorrow's trip."

In a sentimental mood, Jennifer wrapped her arms around Ashlee and Desirae and squeezed their necks until they were all close. "Not going to lie, I don't know where I would be without my girls," Jennifer shared.

"Girl, you know we got you. We'll always be right here," Desirae insisted.

"We stuck like glue," said Ashlee. "Or pieces to the puzzle."

CHAPTER 3
JIGSAW

Bliss

Derek and Jennifer found themselves amidst white sands and radiant blue skies sipping drinks with umbrellas. Days of basking in the sun had tanned Derek's dark hue. Now sun-kissed from having been lost in the moment, Jennifer attempted to take action.

"Babe, can you rub this sunscreen on my back?"

"I can think of a lot of places I could rub on," he replied flirtatiously.

"I could stay here forever. It feels like in the moments, I lose track of time. Hell, sometimes I even forget about my momma." They laughed together.

"Girl, ain't no way you could forget about your momma. Not as much as y'all talk every day. For the life of me, I don't know what you have to talk about that long on the phone."

Jennifer interrupted jokingly, "Wait a minute, don't you be talking about my momma like that."

"You know I love your momma, just like I love you. If it weren't for her, I know you wouldn't know how to cook half of the stuff you do. That's why I stay around."

Jennifer slapped Derek on his shoulder, flinging her sarong to the side, revealing the thick of her thigh and that she was wearing a thong. "Oh, I know you stay around for more than just my cooking."

"Oh, that's how you feel?"

Jennifer seductively nodded her head yes.

"Say less, Mama! Say less! As much as I love being on what feels like a deserted island with you, I can't lie. I'm more than ready to get to the part where we start making little versions of ourselves to run around this sand with us one day," Derek said, sitting up from his lounge chair.

Jennifer laughed in agreement to hide the pain behind her smile. Little did Derek know, she wanted to give him babies more than he wanted them for himself. She mustered up the strength to entice him with words. "Well, maybe we should leave this beach and go try right now." A faint tear rolling down her face on the side that Derek could see dissolved before reaching her chin.

Derek didn't even speak. He immediately began gathering their belongings, even packing Jennifer's bag. Before she knew it, he was standing before her with his hand extended, saying, "Let's go."

By the time they got back to the room, they couldn't keep their hands off one another. Derek even got caught with his hands under Jennifer's sarong and between her thighs as he fingered her on the elevator. They were so connected that they hadn't noticed the elevator door open on their floor to allow other guests to enter.

They laughed like two kids in high school at the notion of being naughty together. Once in their room, Derek pinned Jennifer against the wall, spread her legs with his knee, and slid his fingers inside her. She was so moist; it was clear to Derek how bad Jennifer wanted this moment. He slid his fingers in and out slowly while kissing her slowly. Jennifer could feel his dick becoming harder by the second through his thin beach pants.

"You hear that?" Derek brought Jennifer's attention to the gushy noise of her juices responding to his finger sliding in and out.

Derek removed his finger and raised it to Jennifer's face, who seductively placed it in her mouth and slurped on it as if it was his dick. Derek smirked and told her to turn around. He pressed up against her while taking a second to spit in the palm of his hand. He quickly rubbed his hand along his dick and then inserted it gently into Jennifer's ass.

Startled at first, Jennifer quickly readjusted and relaxed to allow him a smooth entry. Derek gave gentle thrusts at first, giving Jennifer a second to become comfortable. Derek found himself taking random pauses in an attempt to not climax too soon. The wetness of her ass had reached a comparison of what he felt in her pussy.

Jennifer leaned forward, placing more of an arch in her back. She rested her chest against the wall with her arms stretched out above her. She turned her head slightly to catch a glance of the look of weakness displayed on Derek's face. She knew that look. It meant that the end was near. Derek broke eye contact to watch Jennifer's ass wiggle against his pelvis when it hit hard upon contact. In his mind there could be no better view.

Jennifer yelled, "Climb in me!"

Derek was already gripping one of her ass cheeks with one hand while resting the other on her lower back. He felt the ejaculation coming, so he stood up straight while ceasing to thrust and wrapping his arms around her body, cupping her breast. He quickly forced all of himself into her, applying every ounce of pressure behind it that he could find in this moment of complete weakness. Once there was nothing else to give, he pulled out but rested his body against hers.

The sounds of the ocean hitting the sand and Derek struggling to catch his breath was all Jennifer could hear. She turned around, allowing their eyes to connect as they smiled in admiration for each other.

After they made love, Derek got up and ran a hot bath for Jennifer. He wanted to give her a moment to relax before their dinner reservation later that night. Just as he retreated to the sitting area to watch TV, he noticed that his phone was illuminated. Although he had made a habit of placing it face down in Jennifer's presence, the continuous notifications caught his attention. When he picked it up, a text message from a contact Jason Jones read, *Derek. We need to talk. This can't wait.*

What the hell can it be now? he thought to himself. In haste, he selected the contact to dial the number.

As the phone rang, Derek stood back up to walk to the bathroom. "Babe, are you good?"

"Yes, I'm in heaven, Derek. Absolute heaven."

Before he could reply, a voice on the other end of the phone scolded, "Oh so she's in heaven while I'm stuck here, huh? Ain't that a bitch."

He whispered, "Listen to me, Bec. You can't just contact me like this. We've got to move differently. I've told you many times that nobody has to get hurt."

"Looks like that shit ain't working out, 'cause I'm over here hurting. How the fuck do you expect me to have a relationship with my damn self? I can't call, can't text, can't do shit. I'm getting fed up. I honestly don't know how much longer I can do this. At least not like this. Things are changing."

Derek interjected, "Calm the fuck down. I told you when this shit started that I was married and if you were going to fuck with me that you would need to know your place. Now this can be as good or as fucked-up as you want it to be. I was under the impression that we shared something special, but if you want to be the reason shit gets fucked up, then I'm done."

With a total change in demeanor, the woman on the other end of the line spoke. "Wait. No. No. Hold on, baby. I just. I mean. I sometimes get carried away. When we are together, everything is just so perfect. I just need to see you. I need to talk to you."

Derek sat in silence, refusing to reply until she pitifully inquired, "You still there?"

"I'm here. And I hear you. This just has to stop though, for real."

"I understand. Just get back to me when you can, Daddy. I need to feel you inside of me. I need to feel you. I need to touch you."

"Damn, shorty. I want this to work too. We just have to move the way we can move. It's as simple as that. So if we are all good, I'll make sure to get there to see you tomorrow."

"Oh yes, just call me when you get back. I'm ready for you."

"Now that's what I like to hear. Later."

After hanging up abruptly, Derek rolled his eyes toward the back of his head and let out a huge sigh of relief.

"And who are you talking to, Derek? We're out of the country, for goodness sakes."

Derek jumped up, startled. "Oh. Man, babe. That was Jason. Jason Lawson. You probably don't remember him, but we've been working on closing a few deals with him for this expansion."

Jennifer approached wearing only a bath towel. "Babe, you promised no business on this trip, only pleasure.

Besides, tonight is our last night here. I want your memory of it to be special. You deserve that time off."

"Only pleasure," Derek repeated while raising an eyebrow. "You're right, babe. Only pleasure."

Monday Is a State of Mind

When the stainless steel elevator doors opened, Desirae emerged with a vengeance. Her bob was perfectly trimmed to complement the gray fitted dress that flattered her curves perfectly and black Tom Ford pointed pumps. Her heather gray trench coat rested over her arm where she carried her favorite navy Hermes bag. She looked like new money as she strutted into the office. And after her weekend tryst with Malik, she convinced herself that she was invincible.

On this day, she entered the conference room with newfound confidence. It was as if the late nights and early mornings in the bed with Malik redefined who she was or at least how she carried herself. And although the pressure of it all was no different, she was different, and that was what mattered. In her mind, dick on the weekend was good for the soul. She couldn't get the image of his chiseled body against hers out of her mind, but she attempted to focus. While preparing to take her seat in the normal space, third chair from the head of the table on the left side, she was pleasantly surprised by the presence of a new face. Although not new to the firm, he was new to the Monday morning staff meetings.

Before taking her seat, she stopped just before his. "Reggie, what are you doing in here?"

"Well, that's how you welcome a fellow associate? I mean, by the way, you're standing there, you'd think I was opposing counsel," he snarled.

Shifting her demeanor, Desirae replied, "My bad. Don't take it that way. I was just surprised to see you, that's all."

"Good deal. Good deal." He leaned back in the chair, resting his arms on the armrests, and said, "Don't worry. We play for the same team, Queen. I'll always have your back whether you know it or not."

Surprised and somewhat flattered, Desirae shifted her weight to the other hip. "Damn, Reggie. I wasn't expecting that. Thank you."

"I can show you a lot of things you wouldn't expect," he said with a coy voice.

Desirae, now intrigued, smiled and proceeded to her seat.

The door closed as John Wilshire, managing partner, walked in. "All right, all right, ladies and gentlemen, it's time to get to business." His voice, old and creaky yet audacious, sounded like thunder rolling to Desirae. He continued, "I presume you've rested over the weekend, or not. Either way, it's of no concern to me. I am, as you should be, laser-focused on getting us through this next round of briefings in preparation for the hearings as we represent one of the city's most prestigious corporations, best known for their charitable giving to the inner city. We have no other option aside from winning this case. And for some of you, your future with this firm rests on the laurels of this case." He stood at the front of the room, privileged and justifiably so after years of hard-won battles in the courtroom. "That will be all."

The meeting ended as quickly as it began. He hadn't needed to host a long drawn-out moment in time or to express anything other than what he did, which was the importance of winning the case. He demonstrated through his words and demeanor that he expected nothing less for the associates. Desirae, internally shaken and outwardly confident, gathered her belongings to leave the conference room, as did the other associates.

As Desirae approached the door, she noticed a hand in front of her. "Let me get this for you. A woman of your caliber should never have to open her door."

She knew before even turning around that it was Reggie. Stopping just outside of the conference room, they now stood face to face. "You should think about letting me take you out to dinner sometimes," he added.

"Reggie, as much as I would consider your offer, I've learned that it's best to not mix business with pleasure."

"Well, at least I know you think any time spent with me would be pleasurable. I'm on standby if you ever change your mind," he said as he walked past her back to his office. Desirae, who was picking her mouth up from the floor, shook her head and recentered herself before retreating to her office.

Her phone vibrated in her hand. It was a text from Malik that read: *I can still taste you. Don't let too much time pass before I see you again.*

Desirae smiled to herself. "Damn. Some days no one calls and on other days, all the boys want to come out to play. Desirae, what are you going to do with yourself, girl? What are you going to do with yourself?"

Static

Ashlee found herself profusely stirring an oversized pot of homemade sauce amidst a heated exchange on the phone. It was hard to whisper in rage, but she attempted. "I can't do this right now with you, Mom. And the truth is that I've lived my life for everyone else for almost thirty years. It's time I lived for myself now. Out of all the people in the world, I would think that you could understand this."

A snarly voice on the other end replied, "I am aware that it is your life, but you gave that up the minute you became a mother to my grandson. Now you're barely at home because you're working all the time. That is no way to raise a child. You're the mom; you need to spend more time with him."

Ashlee, now fuming, worked intensely to hold it together while putting on her mitts to transfer the sauce to another burner before preparing the pasta.

She slammed the spoon onto the counter and used a cloth attached to her apron to clean her hands before speaking once more. Through her teeth, she uttered, "You are entitled to your opinion, and that's it. As I mentioned, I am at work. I will speak with you later. Please take care."

Ashlee didn't allow her mother to convince her to remain on the phone. She instead said her goodbyes peacefully and ended the call before retreating to the bay window just off the kitchen in hopes of a moment of silence. In that home, it had become her hiding spot when she needed some calm. On some days, she discovered solace and on other days like today, she found herself amidst turmoil in the presence of memories at times too painful to bear.

The moment drew her mind back to her teenage years, where she'd worked relentlessly to hide the truth about her sexuality from her parents. She remembered back to a defining moment standing in her room as a teenager when she mustered up the strength to finally reveal her true self to her parents in hopes of their acceptance. By the time she reached her freshman year, she had managed to maintain a long-term relationship with Edward, who lived on the next street over. They had been inseparable throughout elementary and middle school. They played basketball together and could be seen walking the neighborhood after school and on the weekends, engaging in innocent fun. He was her first kiss and the first person with whom she'd experimented sexually.

By their sophomore year, she'd convinced him that she was ready to relinquish the virginity label. Afterward, nothing was different, except the fact that she wasn't pressed to do it again. All the fireworks that her friends spoke about when describing their first time in the bathrooms while in between classes and at lunch were just not there. She attributed much of it to her and Edward's lack of experience. But they had been friends before lovers, so simply being together was all she cared about, until the day she learned that he had been having regular sex with her next-door neighbor, who held a reputation of being a ho at their school and whose resume was said to include the entire football and basketball team. Too proud to allow herself to be disrespected, she ended their relationship and vowed to take time to discover her sexuality on her terms.

One night after junior prom, she found herself in an empty parking lot talking for hours with Stacy, a recent transfer from New York. Stacy was tall and slender with deep skin. Her jet black shoulder-length hair with bangs framed her wide brown eyes, Ashlee found herself intrigued by them. Lost in the laughter and the moment, Ashlee was compelled to kiss Stacy. Unsure of herself and how Stacy would react, she pulled back in regret. Stacy leaned back onto the driver's side of the car and pulled Ashlee back toward her. Now the aggressor, Stacy kissed Ashlee again. Within five minutes, they were in the backseat of Ashlee's car. Stacy coerced Ashlee to lie back on the seat as she lifted her dress and pulled down her panties. Stacy pleasured Ashlee with her fingers and her mouth until she climaxed. That night,

Stacy introduced Ashlee to a type of pleasure that Edward never had, one she didn't know existed.

From that point forward, Ashlee began to question everything about who she was sexually and her desires. Her truth was that only another girl could make her feel the way her friends described. And the more she became honest with herself, the more she discovered her truth. Beneath it all, she had always known that she was slightly different from her peers. She had never found herself drooling while watching the boys play basketball like her friends, and in the girl's locker rooms, her staring was not a product of comparison, but lust. Before that night with Stacy, she had never allowed herself to acknowledge her feelings as reality, but at that moment, standing in her room, she knew with certainty who she was. And before an attempt to be accepted in the world, she wanted to first discover acceptance at home.

Up to this point, Ashlee had always been an open book, but this was the only chapter that had not been read aloud. Based on her upbringing, Ashlee figured that her father would be accepting of her no matter who or what she decided to be, but it was her mother that would need convincing. Her mother had always maintained a standard in society, one that mirrored the Black family perfected. She demanded that they look a certain way when they left the house and that their home was maintained to a certain standard. Her mother sought approval in status, and her family was expected to rise to the occasion. And although Ashlee knew that confessing to her mother that she was gay was not a part of the perfect plan, she was hoping for acceptance nonetheless. After working up the nerve, she ventured to her parents' room, where she overheard her mother on the phone. With the assumption that it was one of her usual calls with the other cackling hens of the community, she waited just outside the door for the call to end.

Her mother's laugh was infectious, which confirmed that she was gossiping. "Honey, times are changing indeed. These young men are running around here with their pants sagging, and the girls look like little boys. I was at the grocery store the other day and saw a girl was being too touchy with another girl for my comfort."

Noticing Ashlee standing at the doorway, she motioned for her to come into the room.

The lady on the other end of the phone must have agreed with what Ashlee's mom was saying because the next phase of the conversation was a series of "hmmm" and "exactly" before her monologue. "I am neither the judge nor the jury, but I am crystal clear that God made man and woman for a reason. Hell, if he hadn't how would any of us be here?" Noticing that Ashlee had been standing there for quite some time, she put her hand over the phone and said, "What was it, baby? Did you need to tell me something?"

Shaken and convinced by her mother's words that she would never be accepted for who she was, she decided to retreat. "No. No, ma'am. I...I was just checking on you and Daddy."

"Well, your daddy left early to go pick up a few items for the barbecue we're hosting this evening. He will be back shortly."

"Okay, Mom. Sure thing," Ashlee said with her head down. "I guess I'll go pick out something to wear."

"Oh perfect baby, be sure to wear a dress, that's what young ladies do, okay?"

Ashlee nodded her head and began walking back toward her room.

"Like I was saying girl, we've got to teach these children to love and appreciate the way God made them. Half of them are so confused, they don't know who they are anymore." It was at that moment that Ashlee knew she would never be accepted for her truth, so she decided to live a lie.

"I can't wait for my guests to be wowed by your meal tonight," a voice emerged from behind Ashlee.

"Oh yes. They ain't tasted Southern cuisine until they've tasted that shrimp and grits medley that she makes. Ain't that right, baby?" Now there were two voices in conversation with Ashlee, who was lost in thought until pleasantly interrupted.

Ashlee shook her head profusely until she came back to the present. Before she stood her clients Pat and Bridgett, arm in arm. Their long-standing love represented a ray of hope for Ashlee. Pat and Bridgett had been together for over 20 years and managed to defy the odds for same-sex couples at a time when it was far less accepted. Their image of happiness in each other's arms was exactly what Ashlee needed to release her mind from the torment of her past.

"Well, I guess I'd better get back in there and make the magic happen. Keep me posted on the arrival times of the guests, and I'll have everything prepared," Ashlee said as she turned to walk back toward the kitchen. The moment, small yet significant, was a reminder that there was no need to look backward; it was not the direction she was heading toward.

Nostalgia

As the week progressed, Desirae, Ashlee, and Jennifer found their way to each other in a popular bistro in the heart of Midtown. An innocent bystander might assume that the table consisted of three women simply meeting for an early evening dinner, or possibly a friendly exchange amidst a business deal. But to anyone who knew them from their college days, the looks on their faces after consuming their first sip of wine simultaneously revealed a different story.

Although each at different places in their respective lives and levels of maturation, the moments of togetherness, amidst the company of those who understand each other and those willing to relinquish passing of judgment was food that fed their souls. In a society that undermines the bliss that women experience in each other's company, supporting one another, and emotionally stabilizing one another, they had managed to discover the true essence of friendship. From the looks on their faces, neither of them was willing to lose sight of it.

In true Jennifer fashion, she went right to the question that inquiring minds wanted to know. "So, Desirae, how was Miami?"

"Girl, the sex was amazing, like always. I have noticed that I let my limitations get in the way though."

"What limitations?" Ashlee inquired.

"Well, I don't like fingering myself."

"I don't remember you ever saying that. What kind of shit is that?" Jennifer said with her hands in the air. "Umm, so how do you masturbate?"

"Girl, I will use a toy but I don't like touching myself down there," said Desirae.

"Oh, I'm going to have to introduce you to something," Ashlee confidently stated.

"Like what?"

"I'll tell you later."

You could hear Jennifer humming under her breath in disagreement. "But what does this have to do with Malik?"

"He wants to watch me finger myself, but I can't. He gets so frustrated sometimes." Desirae let out a sigh.

Jennifer asked, "Well, what's the problem?"

"I don't know. Just the thought of it makes me squeamish, and I cannot do it. We are wrestling around with him trying

63

to get me to finger myself during sex," Desirae explained while laughing.

Ashlee let out a direct, "Now that is weird but hell, fuck him."

Jennifer interjected, "Period, you are selling yourself short. You are a catch, but you are wasting time with Malik."

Feeling judged, Desirae stated, "I ain't trying to keep Malik's ass. I only deal with him because we just connect on a whole other level sexually. Nothing more between us will ever come."

"You heard her, Jennifer; the dick is suiting her just fine. Plus, I'm still team David," Ashlee asserted.

"And since we're giving confessions, I don't like to be on top during sex either."

Both of the ladies fall back in their chairs. "Oh hell no. Now you are going way too far, Desirae," Ashlee warned.

Desirae laughed. "Girl, when I'm on top, I just want to cover up my whole body. It's just too much attention on me."

"Desirae, you have to loosen up. You're in your head too much. Lord knows I had to learn to let go of my inhibitions the first time I decided to be with a woman. Sex is supposed to be liberating. It's supposed to be the moment when you are set free as opposed to being weighed down."

Jennifer took a sip of her wine. "I'd have to agree with Ashlee. Sex is about connection. And anytime there is a disconnect, then there are other things to consider. As women, how we engage in sex speaks deeply about how we feel about ourselves and our bodies."

"Well now, I know I'm that bitch, so that's not the problem. But I do think that my relationships, in general, are a by-product of some things I haven't healed from," said Desirae.

Jennifer placed her hand on Desirae's arm as a gesture of comfort.

"And that's okay too. We all have some things in our lives that still need to be ironed out. Hell, I know I do. I mean, I haven't even been able to fully be who I am in the presence of my mother," said Ashlee.

"And I haven't even told Derek about my writing because I'm still trying to be a Stepford wife," Jennifer said as she smiled and sighed.

"I do recognize that no relationship is perfect, and our imperfections will often try to steal the show, but I guess I'm more concerned with the fact that I don't even see myself in a relationship with Malik. I only want sex with him. There must be something wrong with me, right?"

Ashlee proclaimed, "Girl, ain't shit wrong with you because you like a good dick. Hell, even I've had some in my lifetime, so I know what you mean. I just don't want any more of it." Ashlee's comedy sent the table bursting into laughter.

"You had some, all right. You almost got these hands because of it too," Jennifer said.

"Oh Lord, here she goes with this story again," Ashlee said as she rolled her eyes.

"You remember it, Desirae, right? The story of how I met Ashlee while we were at Howard University?"

"Girl, how could I forget? You were waiting for your boyfriend outside of the dorm, but he never came down. After over 45 minutes had passed, you decided to sneak up the back stairwell of the building to pay a visit to his room."

Ashlee interrupted, "Do we need to tell this story again?"

"We sure do, it's hysterical," Jennifer said while nodding her head for Desirae to continue.

"As I was saying, by the time you managed to sneak up to the room, you noticed a girl (Ashlee) sitting outside of his door. Now pissed, you walked with haste over to her to ask her what the hell she was doing outside of your man's door."

Ashlee interjected, "But I was just sitting there. There was no need for Jennifer to confront the way she did."

"I sure as hell did. It had only been a few months of being with him and I could just feel that he was up to something. But before then I couldn't prove it."

Desirae continued, "That part. So when you were face to face with Ashlee, you confronted her. Ashlee's response was to stand up and say, 'Babygirl, I don't want him and you're wasting your time.'"

"Oh my God! I wanted to drag you so bad, that was until the door opened and I saw his tired ass standing there adjusting his clothes while some ho in a tight pink dress slid through the narrow space between Ashlee and me. Ashlee looked me squarely in the eyes and said, 'See, you're wasting your time' before turning to walk away with her friend."

"Damn," said Desirae. "The entire time that you were outside waiting on his trifling ass, he was getting it in with some other girl, while Ashlee kept watch at the door. And Ashlee, who signed you up to be the damn lookout anyway?"

"At the time, that was my girl, Marley Washington. I'll never forget that moment. I knew then that I couldn't be cool with someone who was okay with sleeping with other women's men."

Desirae continued, "So like two days later, Jennifer was sitting alone in the school cafeteria, and you walked over to her and said, 'So, are you still with that lame or not?'"

"Bitch, all I could do was laugh. Ashlee laughed in return and from that moment on we became inseparable until that group project landed us at the library, and we found you, Desirae!"

"But of course. You know me, studying as usual. Oh yeah, and Ash and I knew that you would be the perfect fit for that project on entertainment law that we had to figure our way through."

"All I knew was that you made straight As, and Jennifer and I were struggling to get by. Our grades were on the line with that project."

"But who knew that you would be so cool? Now look at us, you can't pry us apart with a stick," said Desirae.

"You've got that right. I wish somebody would try to come between our friendship. Forget what society says about Black women not getting along, our friendship is built to last."

"I want to propose a toast to real love. Jennifer, you, and Derek are the real thing. I mean fuck the bullshit, y'all make love look good. If it weren't for the two of you, I don't know that I would even believe love was out there."

"I'll drink that," Ashlee interjected.

"So cheers, ladies. Cheers to real love. May we know it to be real and may we keep seeking it in our hearts. And happy early anniversary to two of our faves...Jennifer and Derek. May you have many more years of bliss to come."

"Here, here," Jennifer said in agreement as they lifted their glasses and joined them together before drinking. As the night grew old, three women in a bistro became the definition of friendship. Their exchange embodied the notion that friends are the keepers of secrets and souls.

CHAPTER 4

SLOTS

"Yo. Ash. What's good?" Will vibrantly exclaimed from the other end of the phone. Ashlee didn't speak; she only listened. "I'm putting together a last-minute get-together at my house tonight. I need to see if you can be our chef. You know how much my people love your food."

Standing at the intersection of Piedmont and Roswell Road with a French vanilla almond milk latte in one hand and the hand of her most prized possession with the other, Ashlee propped the phone between her neck and shoulder and looked down at her son before responding.

Before she could, Will was already soliciting her response. "Are you there? We've got to get this show on the road. I know these folk will be hungry when they arrive. I've got some heavy hitters coming in for this evening. Truth be told, they could even be clients for you in the future."

Needing to decide in a split second that could result in immediate income and pursuit of purpose, Ashlee was torn. As easy as it all seemed, choosing between her son

69

and work was complicated. Stuttering, she replied, "What time would you need me to be there?"

A voice from below now spoke. "Mommy, what time are we going to the park?"

Clasping her lips together and mumbling under her breath was all that she could do. "SHIT." Frustrated at the moment, Ashlee fought back the frustration in the presence of her son. "Just a minute, baby. Mommy has to take this work call." She went back to the phone. "Sure thing. I'll be right over."

"Bet. You always come through when I need you. Thanks," he said before ending the call.

Ashlee immediately called Xavier. "Hey, Xavier. I need a favor. Can you get Nolan for me? I have a job that I need to take, and it was short notice."

"Sure, are you bringing him here or you want me to meet you at your place?"

"Meet me at my place and you can stay there. That way he can be in his bed when I get in tonight."

"Bet. I'll be there in 20."

"Thanks."

Ashlee hung up and looked down at her son with guilt in her eyes. "Change of plans, babe. Daddy is going to take you to the park instead of Mommy." She hugged him as tightly as she could until the guilt exited through her eyes in the form of tears.

Smoke & Mirrors

In a quaint restaurant in Buckhead, Jennifer sat nestled in a pink oversized cardigan and black leggings near the back corner, defined by a white brick wall. The silver sequence on the cover of her notebook formed the letter J, and a matching pen with a feather extending from the top couldn't be missed. Noticeably engaged with her writing, she hardly heard the waitress stop by to offer her a glass of water while she awaited her guest. The more she wrote, the more the words seemed to flow from her pen. She was almost in a trance-like state until she noticed a set of black lace-up heels standing below her table. She slowly glanced up to recognize a familiar face.

"Lisa! Oh my God, I'm so glad you could make it. Sit down, sit down," she said as she gestured at the other seat. "Are you hungry?"

"Actually, I'm not too hungry. I had a meeting up in Marietta just before coming to meet you."

Jennifer ignored her statement. "Girl, let's get you some food." She motioned for the waitress to return. "You know this is the South, and honey, if there is one thing that we do, it's feeding people." They laughed together.

"How long has it been now since you moved from New York to Atlanta?"

"It is crazy how fast the time has flown. I've been here for a year now already."

"Time does fly, but I must say Atlanta suits you. You wouldn't think that a girl from the Bronx would leave New York to become a writer in Atlanta. That's almost unheard of, but I must say, things are progressing nicely here. And look at you. You look amazing. Tan much?"

Blushing, Jennifer replied, "I am just getting back from Turks and Caicos with Derek."

"Wow. Turks and Caicos! How was it?"

"Girl, it was absolute paradise. I wasn't ready to come back to Atlanta or to return to work."

"I hear that. From the looks of things, you guys spent quite a bit of time in the sun. I'm here for it, honey."

"Okay, girl. My melanin is poppin," Jennifer exclaimed as she tilted her head to the side to show off her skin.

"So did you get any writing done while you were there? It seems like the perfect place to be inspired." Jennifer dropped her head. "What? I mean it's okay if you didn't. You were on a whole vacation."

"Girl, it's not that I wasn't inspired. The truth is that I would have loved to have sat on the beach and poured my heart onto the paper. I just couldn't."

"What do you mean you couldn't? Was it that your guys were too busy? I know excursions can take up a lot of time as well." Now concerned, Lisa awaited Jennifer's response.

"This is exactly why I wanted to meet you today. I needed to talk to someone who understands the mind of a writer. I've been hiding my writing from everyone, especially

Derek. Somehow, I have made up my mind that being a writer and going full-time with my blog is outside of the realm of possibility for a wife like me."

"Okay, girl, now you know you've got to give me more than that. What exactly do you mean when you say 'a wife like you'?"

Jennifer took a deep breath before speaking. "I just mean I'm working hard to be what I think Derek wants and needs, and we're thinking about starting our family together, and I just don't want to add any stress by attempting to launch a career that could or could not fare well in the end just because it's what I'm passionate about. Passionate does not pay the bills."

"Well, I can't blame you for feeling anxious about becoming a full-time writer. This shit is not for the faint of heart, I'll be the first to admit that, but I don't want you to forget that what you seek is seeking you. You're a writer through and through, and it's not something that you will ever be able to shake, it's in your DNA. All things considered, writing needs you, and you need it. I mean, can you look me in my eyes and tell me with a straight face that writing doesn't set your soul on fire?"

"I can't. There is no way for me to deny how much I love it. The question is, would the pursuit of it be worth the risk?"

"You remind me of myself before taking the leap of faith to come to Atlanta. To leave a place like New York as a writer feels like a career suicide. All of the literary agents, publications, and industry icons are there. Coming to Atlanta was more about me learning to recognize my own strength than it was about what anyone else would think about my choice to do so. I also learned that what God has for you is already yours, and no one can change that. Now if you were a lousy writer, this conversation would be going in a different direction, but I've seen your skills. Hell, I'm probably the first one on the blog every morning in search of some of that good old-fashioned empowerment that you serve up daily."

"Girl, you've got me blushing over here," Jennifer said.

"At the end of the day, you won't ever know which doors will open for you unless you are willing to turn the handle."

"You're right, and I thank you from the bottom of my heart for being a sounding board and source of inspiration. I already know for a fact that you'll be on the cover of Essence someday. Your following has grown so much in the last year. The whole world is listening to you," Jennifer encouraged.

"I do what I do for the culture. Nothing more, nothing less," Lisa said with a huge smile on her face. "And so shall you, Queen."

Lisa lifted her glass and nodded for Jennifer to lift hers. "Here's to writing that pays the bills!"

"And I'll drink to that," said Jennifer with newfound hope in her eyes.

Happiness, Whatever That Means

Later that night after finishing the dinner with Will, Ashlee nervously pulled up to the restaurant that she had agreed to meet at for her date. Greeted by the valet, she looked in the mirror once more to make sure her hair wasn't flat before exiting her car. Upon arrival at the hostess stand, she was greeted by a leggy waitress dressed in all black with pale skin, buzzed rainbow hair, and a nose ring.

"Hi. I'm here to meet someone who is already seated," Ashlee told her.

"Dinner with friends tonight, is it?" the waitress inquired.

"Actually, this is kind of a first date."

With eyebrows raised, the waitress responded, "I understand. First dates are always special. I'm happy to help you find your table. Can you tell me what he looks like?"

Lowering her head slightly before responding, Ashlee murmured, "Actually, it's she."

The waitress gasped slightly, leaving her mouth open in the absence of a sensible response. Ashlee couldn't help but notice the look on her face. It was a look she had seen before but one that she had learned to overcome. She'd made up in her mind after the relationship ended with her son's father that she would refrain from placing constraints of labels on her personal life. Should love choose to find her, she no longer cared that the prospect might be in the arms of another woman.

Before she could speak another word, Ashlee saw a hand waving in the distance. "I see her right over there. Thanks for all of your help though," she said sarcastically before rolling her eyes and heading to seat herself.

Tai, a rich hue of caramel with short coiffed hair almost the same color, petite in stature, and dressed in a black blazer with the sleeves rolled at the bottom and a white button-down shirt underneath, sat at a table near a window toward the back of the restaurant awaiting Ashlee. Ashlee secretly hoped that her first attempt at online dating would work out. As she got closer to the table, her smile grew.

"You must be Tai. I'm Ashlee," she said, extending her hand across the table to shake her hand.

Tai stood up and walked around the table toward Ashlee, opening her arms wide. "Ashlee, I'm a hugger."

Ashlee smiled a bit shyly and stepped into Tai's embrace. In the newness of the moment, they held each other just long enough for Ashlee to know with certainty that she wanted to stay. Although she was starting over with love, she was open to new beginnings and even the prospect of new sexual exploits, this time with a woman.

No Justice, No Peace

Desirae spent the entire day at the kitchen table, which was covered in papers from the briefing for the upcoming court case, some spilling onto the floor. From the look in her eyes, she didn't have it all figured out, although the rest of the world expected her to. The anxiety in her face was concerning, and a sign of her desperation to seem knowledgeable in front of her peers. The prospect of making partner at the firm was so close that she could feel it. Becoming an equal with the men who'd hired her was her chase of destiny. Behind the scenes, no one saw how hard she worked. The countless hours, the bills still cutting into her paycheck from years of college and training for the LSAT were remnants and reasons why she was deserving. Moments of intensity made her question what it had all been for. From the look in her eyes, she didn›t have it all figured out.

A knock at the door woke her from her slumber. Startled, she jumped and lifted her head from the table. Before she could begin walking to the door, a bold series of knocks ensued. She could hear the person on the other side demanding that she open the door.

"Desirae. Desirae. Girl, I know you don't have me standing out here waiting on you to open the door. You knew I was coming."

Desirae reached for the door with anticipation of what would be. Slowly swinging the door open, she saw a familiar face.

"Girl. What kind of hospitality are you offering up?" A short, stout woman with wiry salt and pepper coils, a hint of red lipstick atop thin lips, and a red suit and black patent leather flats came walking in. Desirae noticed a purple carry-on with a pink ribbon tied around it trailing behind her. "I've never heard of this sending a car to pick someone up. In my day, when someone was coming to visit you, you were standing right there to pick them up yourself. My how times have changed."

"Indeed. Times have changed," Desirae rebutted.

After securing her luggage by the door, the woman demanded, "Well. Let me look at you" as she motioned for Desirae to spin around to allow her to give a solid look over before replying with her analysis. "From the looks of this place and you, I'd say you're a little in over your head."

Offended, Desirae replied, "Well it's not easy to work your fingers to the bone day and night to chase a dream that nobody can see except you."

"To whom much is given, much is required, little girl."

"Well, that may be true, but let's be clear, I wasn't given anything."

"Who are you talking to?" She looked around. "Now you may not have had everything you wanted, but you had the very best of everything you needed. You had a roof over your head, clothes on your body, and food to eat. I'd say that's a lot," the woman replied.

Silence filled the room. Desirae knew better than to talk back, but there was so much she wanted to say. For so many years she'd had pent-up frustration that if left unresolved could prove to be detrimental.

Instead of firing back, Desirae clasped her lips together, tilted her head, and took a big, cleansing breath to calm her nerves. She had learned the technique in a yoga class she'd taken when studying for the LSAT to calm her anxiety and had been using it in stressful situations ever since. When she gathered herself, she managed to utter pleasantries in exchange for the spewing that had been thrown her way. "You know what, why don't you let me get you a bottle of water and I can show you to your room to sit for a bit. I know you must be tired from traveling."

The woman looked over at the table where Desirae had been at war with the papers and said, "Mmmmhhh. I guess that would be nice. Looks like you need a moment to pull yourself together."

"Indeed, I do," Desirae rebutted as she walked towards the refrigerator. "I placed a basket in your room with a towel, washcloth, and eye mask if you'd like to lie down for a bit. I will add your water there as well."

"A nice hot shower sounds like a good idea. I want to wash off the germs of all those nasty folks on the plane before I sit on the bed or anywhere else for that matter." She looked up at Desirae and shook her head before retreating to the spare bedroom in Desirae's condo.

"I'll let you get settled in. Let me know if you need anything," Desirae said in a faint voice as she closed the door behind her. Instead of returning to the table, she sank to the floor just outside the door and overwhelmed by the memories of growing up under the stern hand of a woman who was so heavily opinionated. Desirae loved her mother, but even in her presence, she felt that she was left to navigate the world alone. No one truly understood her. And although the world saw Desirae as strong, she often succumbed to what felt like weakness even if only for brief moments at a time. She took a huge sigh and exhaled everything that told her to stay there in her emotions. She recognized that the court would not take into consideration the fact that she was on the verge of an emotional breakdown. The men at the firm were not concerned with her emotional well-being, only results. That alone forced her to wipe her tears and to peel herself from the floor to move back to the table flanked with papers from the briefing.

And there she sat, reading, and writing, thinking, and replaying the series of events surrounding the case over and over again until she realized that it was dark outside. Her mother had fallen asleep, but Desirae wanted to ensure she ate dinner. She began assembling the food she'd ordered from Gladys Knight's Chicken & Waffles earlier in the day on the countertop. It was her mother's favorite, and she requested it every time she came to visit.

After she woke her mother up for dinner, they sat together amidst the papers, laughing about old times. It was a rare occasion where they simply enjoyed each other's company without struggle or strife. The time in her mother's company proved to serve as a remembrance of love and healing for Desirae's wounded soul.

Fun Distractions

Jennifer was standing in the doorway of the living room observing Derek stretched out on the sofa watching the game, beer in one hand and his other resting inside his sweats. Jennifer walked into the room, and when she was a foot away from him, she lifted her sundress to her thighs and dropped to her knees. Derek glanced away from the TV and locked eyes with her. She moved in closer, parting his legs with her hands but never losing eye contact.

Derek smirked, feeling his dick enlarge with the excitement of what was to come. Jennifer slid his shirt up and began to kiss and lick his stomach, stopping right above his pants.

Derek said, "Take what you want."

She slipped his dick out of his pants and immediately slid her tongue against it, starting from the bottom of the shaft and gliding up to the top. Once she reached the top, she devoured his dick while making a swallowing motion with her throat when she felt the tip reach the back of her mouth.

Derek let out a soft moan while closing his eyes and letting his head drop back. He grabbed Jennifer's hair as she went up and down on his dick. Keeping a tight grip with her mouth while massaging his dick with her tongue, she could feel Derek making slight circular motions with his pelvis, going with her rhythm of sucking.

Her sucking left a collection of spit in her mouth, and when she reached the top of his dick, she allowed it to slowly drip from her mouth to his dick. As they held eye contact, Jennifer went back down Derek's dick, taking it all in while making a side-to-side motion with her head as she moved up and down.

Derek leaned forward and slid Jennifer's straps off her shoulder. He slipped his hands inside the dress and skimmed them down her back to her butt. He gave her a gentle slap on the ass while encouraging her to keep going by whispering the words, "You're my slut, right?"

This aroused Jennifer more, and she began massaging his balls with her hands while continuing to suck on his dick.

Derek slid his hand between her cheeks, gliding his finger past her anus and landing at her vagina. He glided his finger against her pussy, feeling her sweet juices resting on his fingers. To give him a better angle, Jennifer leaned lower, taking Derek's balls in her mouth and massaging them with her tongue. Derek slipped his finger inside of her, sliding it in and out slowly, enjoying the slippery noise that her pussy made. Jennifer moved back and forth between his balls, becoming sloppier and sloppier with her sucking as more saliva collected in her mouth.

Derek leaned back on the sofa while tasting the finger that he'd removed from inside of Jennifer. She pushed his balls closer to his dick, creating a clearing to his gooch. Slipping her tongue a little lower to his anus, she began tickling it. Derek let out a high-pitched moan, biting his lower lip as she slid her tongue upward to his gooch, caressing it before going back to his dick. Then she went back to sucking his penis, rotating from slow and gentle to a hard and fast motion. Derek grabbed her hair to signal he was going to nut soon. Jennifer kept pace, continuing even when feeling Derek's dick pulsate inside of her mouth as she swallowed his creamy seed. Derek screamed out a loud "Fuck!" as he lost all life in his body. Jennifer moved up to lay on the sofa, getting a passionate kiss from Derek as she settled comfortably beside him.

Derek's phone vibrated where it lay, on the opposite side of Jennifer. After giving a slide glance to ensure that Jennifer was not looking, Derek slid the message open to read: *When are you coming by? I miss you and your pussy needs you!*

CHAPTER 5

TABS

Cold War

Running late for her morning run with David, Desirae jogged through the main entrance of Piedmont Park. In an attempt to keep her momentum going, she blasted her favorite playlist, which was filled with Jeezy, Drake, and Lil Wayne. As she made her way to the main track, she began to scan the area for David, eventually finding him standing on the side looking at his phone.

As she got closer, she removed her headphones and slowed down to an even pace. "Hey, sorry I'm late. I had some last-minute things come up this morning," she whispered as she brushed her hand across his ass in an attempt to startle him.

David jumped but quickly recognized her voice. He turned to hug her and gave her a gentle kiss. "I understand. I know it can be hectic."

They both stepped to the side to stretch in the nearby grass.

"How was your week?" Desirae asked while taking in the astonishing view of David's muscular physique.

After noticing her examining his body, David responded, "It was good. I closed on a few deals and had the chance to look at a good investment property. I keep telling you to let me help you look into some properties."

"I know, I know. I have way too much on my plate right now. I can't add anything else at the moment."

"You do realize you make life harder than it has to be."

Irritated with the direction the conversation was going, Desirae took off running while asking the question, "What does that mean?"

Caught off guard by her actions, David ran after her. Finally catching up, he explained, "All I'm saying is you don't have to do everything alone."

"Well, I thrive in being independent. I'm not about to shrink myself to make someone else feel comfortable."

"What the hell does that have to do with what I just said?"

Feeling frustrated, Desirae continued to run, ignoring his question.

David followed up with, "Desi! Desi!" forcing her to come to an abrupt stop.

"What? You know how I feel about having these conversations," Desirae shouted.

"It's really sad. You are so cold that you are legit handling me as if me wanting to love you is a bad thing."

"Well, I don't understand why you have to make things so difficult. We're in a good space and we're enjoying each other. Is that not enough?"

"No, it's not!" David proclaimed.

Noticing that people had heard their raised voices, David motioned for Desirae to join him on some near-by stone steps. "It's not enough for me. You are beautiful, smart, and ambitious. All things I love about you. But that can't be it to you and us."

"It's not. I really like you. You are the break I need from my reality."

David let out a deep sigh. "You say that all the time, but your actions contradict your words. You are cold. It's like no matter how much I try to break through, you won't let me in." He stood up. "Look at you now. I'm saying all of this, and you are unbothered."

Desirae held her hand out. "Can you lower your voice and come sit back down?"

David took her hand and resettled on the steps next to her. A few people ran by, so they sat in silence, giving each other time to breathe.

"I honestly don't know what to say, David."

With noticeable defeat, David stated, "We have been do-ing this dance for over a year now. I have been very clear with how I feel about you and how I see you in my future."

Desirae nodded. "You have, and I appreciate you for be-ing vulnerable and transparent with me."

"Desi, I'm 33 years old, no kids, financially stable, no dra-ma, ambitious, and I am open to love and being in a serious relationship."

Using her hands for emphasis, she said, "Okay, I know you're a catch if that's where this is going."

"Well, I need you to act as you know. If we are going to continue what we're doing, we have to get serious or...."

Desirae interjected, "Or what, call it quits?"

David nodded anxiously with tension in his eyes, which prompted Desirae to stare off into space for a minute, clearly collecting her thoughts.

After a few moments, David broke the silence. "Damn, Desi, why are you making it so damn hard? I want you! I want this to work."

Desirae stood up with conviction, opened David's contact information on her phone, and blocked him. She turned to him with certainty in her eyes and calmly stated, "But this is not going to work for me. I wish you well, and I know you will find the right woman. I'm just not her." Putting her headphones in her ears, she began to run again, leaving David sitting on the steps.

Imperfectly Perfect

Jennifer and Derek were cuddled on the sofa, with Derek watching television and Jennifer resting against him looking through a magazine. Derek was not fully paying attention since he was watching an intense basketball game, but Jennifer continued with the conversation.

"Can you imagine how different our life will be once we have a baby?" Jennifer asked, but Derek did not respond, prompting her to shove her elbow into his chest to get his attention.

"I haven't thought about it," he finally mumbled.

Jennifer continued. "I wonder if the baby will look more like you or me. Hopefully, me." She chuckled.

Becoming irritated, Derek responded, "I don't know. It doesn't matter, your shit doesn't work."

Jennifer sat in silent disbelief. Did the man she loved just utter words that were horrific and beyond heartbreaking? At that moment Jennifer might have had a life partner, but she felt alone in this fight to conceive. Getting up from the sofa, she left the room. Derek sat in place watching the game with no recognition of the hurt he'd just caused.

Days passed, and Jennifer carried Derek's words with her. She found herself asking, how could the man she thought was sent by God have been so insensitive to her pain? How could he not see the heaviness that the absence of a baby was causing her? Was there a disconnect between them that she had not noticed before?

Derek, feeling uncomfortable with the cold hugs and empty words, decided to approach her. He found her in the bathroom putting on makeup. "It's time to check in," he said in a gentle but firm manner while closing the bathroom door behind him.

They had an understanding that "check-in time" was when one of them felt that something needed to be addressed, and it was safe to be completely honest at that moment.

Derek looked at Jennifer in the mirror and asked, "What is going on?"

Jennifer took a deep breath while trying to decide how to put words to what she felt. Kneeling down, she pulled the box of used pregnancy tests from the back of the sink cabinet and placed it on the bathroom sink in front of Derek, waiting for his response.

Derek searched through the box, looking at what seemed to be twenty pregnancy tests, all showing negative results. Finally he looked up from the box to find Jennifer looking at him with shame written on her face. Tears began to roll down her cheeks.

"This is what's wrong with me. Months of trying to get pregnant. I'm broken! What kind of woman am I if I cannot give you a child? Every single day I am reminded how amazing it is to bring life into this world, and as your wife that is something I cannot do."

Derek stood in silence, taken aback by what his wife had shared. As he watched the pain flow from her eyes, he began to cry himself, feeling that he had failed his wife. How could he have missed the opportunity to be his wife's strength in a time that she felt so weak? How could he have allowed time to pass with his wife feeling alone when they'd vowed to conquer the world together? Not to forget, his acts of betrayal were weighing on him like blocks of concrete heavy with guilt.

Derek pulled Jennifer into his arms and embraced her as she cried. He whispered to her, "I'm sorry that I was not there for you when you needed me to be."

Jennifer lifted her head and Derrick put a finger under her chin so that they were facing eye to eye. "We are going to figure this out, and regardless of what happens, I got you. You are not broken, you are perfect. Perfectly made for me."

Nobody Wins When the Family Feuds

The drive through the winding rows of trees that seemingly formed columns at the edges of the road gave the illusion of a vineyard.

Will managed to do well for himself as a CPA at an investment firm in Atlanta. Somewhat of a genius, he'd finished college at 19 years old and found a firm willing to take a chance on a raw, young, energetic talent. Now a vet in the numbers game, he oversaw accounts of the city's most prominent sports athletes, their agents, and the heavy hitters in the business sector. Both his salary and affluence came with a bevy of perks, which often led to an overflow of women and privilege in the city. Not only did those around him benefit from it, but many became better for it.

By the time Ashlee got to the door, Will was already standing just outside of it taunting her. "Lemme see what you got for us today, girl."

Ashlee was at the trunk of her car, loading bags on her arms as far back as they could go in a desperate attempt to make a single trip into the house. "Instead of standing there doing all that talking, you can come on out here and help with these bags," Ashlee called.

"Ha! I knew you were about to say that. You know I got you." Will walked away from the black wrought iron doors and met Ashlee halfway, retrieving the bags from her arms.

Before Ashlee could get to work, she had no choice but to engage in a big brother little sister chat with Will. Whether he acknowledged it publicly or not, he had enlisted Ashlee as his sounding board. She was now his confidant. And the times that she cooked for him were more like impromptu counseling sessions in the kitchen.

"And where shall I sit today?" he inquired while placing the groceries on top of the counter.

"Sit? Sit for what? I know you are not trying to come in here and keep me from getting started again to talk about these women you rotate in and out of this house like a revolving door."

"Damn girl, not a revolving door. I like to think of it as seasons. They say that every person that comes into your life is there for a season."

"Well, these are some short-ass seasons if you ask me." They laughed together as Ashlee began to unpack the items she picked up from the store and prep the seasonings. Pulling out a small menu card from her apron, she said, "Go on then. What is it that you want to talk about today?"

"Well, first I need to tell you that we will have about 10 people coming tonight. The food is going to be the most important detail because some of these people are a little obnoxious. They don't really attend events like this to socialize; they are more focused on closing deals. I need the food to keep them at bay while I make my rounds."

She interjected, "Are we talking rounds with your personal lady friends or rounds with the prospective clients?"

With his hands flailing in the air, he said, "Ashlee, I'm talking about the clients."

"Well, I thought I'd clarify. You never know in this house."

"Back to what I was saying before you interrupted me. I also need to be able to get in a little quality time with Nadia. She's coming, and I don't want her to feel left out."

Ashlee stopped in her tracks. "Wait, so is this getting serious? I must admit, I've never heard you talk about anyone this often. And if I'm not mistaken, there is something in your eyes when you mention her name. Wait...Do you love her?"

"I mean, I'll be the first to admit that love is a stretch for me, but I'm sure it's inside of me somewhere. But what I can say is that I think about her a lot. She is who I get excited about when she calls. I haven't felt like this about anyone in my entire adult life."

"Damn, Will. I think you're falling for her. What's so special about her? I mean no shade, it's just that you've had your fair share of women to choose from."

"You tell no lies, Ash, but the truth is there is no logical reason that I can pinpoint. I can only tell you how I feel." Rubbing his hands over his beard and appearing to be in deep thought, he said, "To be honest, no one has ever held my attention for that long. It seems that over time, I get bored, but it hasn't happened yet."

"Yet. Does that mean that you anticipate it to happen?" Ashley interrogated.

"No. No. I don't mean that I think it will, it just always does."

"So if you never get bored with her and you always want to be around her, does that mean that you would be willing to do what it takes to keep her around permanently?"

"Damn, Ash, you're going too deep today. I can only wrap my mind around this current moment. I honestly can't say what the future holds."

"Okay okay," Ashlee replied in kind.

"And what about you, Ash? Have you ever had someone that held your attention in a way that no one else could?"

Ashlee paused before answering, considering if she would disclose the entire truth or give him the filtered version of her thoughts. "I would love to tell you that I felt that way during my marriage to Xavier, and in the beginning, I did. I was cooking and cleaning, and washing clothes, making sure the house was clean, and that I kept myself up for my marriage. I didn't want to feel like things would not work because of something that I didn't do. I vowed to give it my all. I literally worshipped the ground that man walked on. Most importantly, we were best friends so it was easy to be around him and easy for me to love him."

"Damn, that sounds like a perfect relationship," Will interjected.

Nodding her head in disagreement, she said, "It may sound perfect to you, but it was far from that because, in the process of loving him, I lost the ability to love myself. When you're focused on pouring into everyone else, eventually your well runs dry."

Will leaned his back against the wall as if perplexed. "I guess I never really thought about it that way. To be honest, I've never heard a woman speak on the issue. The women I've dealt with want to rush into marriage, but I know they see me as a meal ticket, and I don't allow them to get too close."

"And I can understand that. I just pray that whoever you do allow to hold your heart is willing to protect it at all costs. You're one of the good ones, Will."

"You aren't too bad yourself there, Ashlee."

Ashlee smiled, thankful for the exchanges that were now becoming a regular occurrence with Will as they were just as fruitful for her as they were for him. "Well, now that we have your mind clear for the next few hours, let me work my magic in this kitchen. Get out!"

"Say less, sis. Glad you're here."

"Always," Ashlee said with an oversized smile.

As Will left the kitchen, Ashlee hurried to finish prepping the meal and make up for the lost time devoted to Will's debriefing. "Alexa, play Summer Walker."

The sound of her voice was soothing and allowed her to get lost in creating an edible masterpiece for Will's event. Her mind was led back to the question she'd posed to Will. Would he be willing to do what it takes to keep love around permanently?

She began to reflect on the first time she'd fallen in love with another woman. Cynthia was reserved and academically astute. She'd practically lived at the library, and on occasions could be identified by her lengthy, lean legs and Doc Martin boots under the oversized oak study tables. Although much more subdued, she mimicked a make-up-less Kerry Washington.

A chance group assignment that placed them together had proven to be the glue. As the only two Black girls in the group, they found themselves discovering commonalities amidst the hidden bias rendered by their counterparts. They discovered synergy that turned into extended study hours and increased time together when one of the group members dropped out, leaving them with an additional share of coursework.

Even after the group project came to an end, they kept in touch, spending most of their free time together. Cynthia became a significant part of the reason Ashlee conquered some of her hardest courses. Their friendship turned into mutual love and respect, which led to intimacy. Now, sure of herself and more open to exploring sexually, Ashlee recognized that she felt most pleasure with women as opposed to men. And because neither Ashlee nor Cynthia had many partners, they found themselves free to experiment and explore their sexual desires together.

Although neither formally confirmed their relationship, those close to the pair on campus could conclude that they were far more than friends. The more time they spent together, the more comfortable they got with the idea of not hiding their relationship from the rest of the world. One night while out at dinner, Ashlee told Cynthia that she was in love with her. Without hesitation, Cynthia said it back. And from that night forward, they discussed building a life together after college and vowed to remain committed to enhancing their love.

One evening when Ashlee returned home for a routine visit, she found herself engulfed in a heart-wrenching conversation with her parents about making sound decisions for her career and life after college. And although they hadn't said the words, there was a subliminal expectation for her to get a good job, become a wife, and start a family. They'd positioned her to achieve the American Dream according to their philosophy. The mounting pressure and Ashlee's desire to please her parents led her to make the heart-wrenching decision to end her relationship with Cynthia. Her decision was the beginning of the end for their relationship and her power to love the way she saw fit. In her heart, she knew that Cynthia should have been the one that she should have fought to keep permanently. She couldn't help but wonder what life would be like if she had only been true to who she was back then.

Ashlee was startled, and her thoughts were disrupted by the sound of Will's voice. "Ash, I can't wait for you to meet her."

"Damn, you scared me."

Will tapped the wall and walked to the foyer to meet with the staff in preparation for the evening. Ashlee stood with her hands placed upon the cutting board, wondering if she would ever be able to find love as she had once experienced and the kind that created the excitement that Will displayed again. Only time would tell.

Sometimes Tough Love Is the Answer

Jennifer was standing in the kitchen prepping for the night festivities. The food for the night was spread out amongst the kitchen island, to include the ingredients to make homemade Rice Crispy treats, three wine glasses, a bottle of Ménage à Trois, and Welch's sparkling juice for Jennifer.

Ashlee rejoined Jennifer in the kitchen after calling to check on Nolan.

"Is everything okay?" Jennifer asked after noticing the flustered look on Ashlee's face.

"No, but it will be."

"What happened?"

"Xavier took Nolan to meet his girlfriend after we had already agreed that he would wait a little bit longer."

Puzzled by Ashlee's statement, Jennifer asked, "I thought you liked the girl?"

"She's okay, but she and Xavier do not see eye to eye about a few things that are major things; therefore, don't bring Nolan into that until he knows it's going to work long term."

In an effort to ease the tension, Jennifer poured Ashlee a glass of wine and the Welch's juice for herself. "So how are you going to handle it?"

"I've already said what I needed to say for the moment. He will get the rest of my energy when I get home."

"Well, don't go kill the man. Hear him out too."

"Of course I'm going to listen. But what's not going to happen is him messing up the co-parenting relationship we've worked so hard to establish."

"I understand," Jennifer responded as she pulled the cold ingredients from the refrigerator.

"Where is Derek?"

"Oh, he went out. He's always with Jeremy on Fridays."

Ashlee took a sip of wine from her glass before saying, "Every Friday?"

Pretending to ignore the insinuation behind the question, Jennifer responded, "Yep, and if I'm not with y'all, that's when I have some me-time." While mixing the ingredients in a bowl, she continued, "You have to have time apart sometimes. It definitely helps us remain sane."

"Okay now, let me find out you are putting on for me and clocking him."

"Absolutely not! I trust him. We went through what we went through in college, and that's where we left it. And besides, he's changed and wouldn't dare mess what we have up."

The girls were interrupted by the doorbell ringing several times. Ashlee rushed to the door to appease Desirae's lack of patience. Desirae walked into the kitchen with a look of frustration and exhaustion, quickly dropping her purse on the counter and taking a seat at the island.

"Pour me a glass now," she demanded.

Jennifer and Ashlee shared a puzzled look. "Umm, what's up with you?"

"Every damn thing at this point."

Placing a full glass of wine in front of Desirae, Jennifer affirmed, "Start from the top."

"Work is work, which is a lot. Mr. Walshire is expecting perfection from the candidates for partner."

"Is he asking for perfection or are you creating that narrative yourself?" Jennifer asked.

"Hell, I don't know! I feel so much pressure and anxiety. Everything I've been doing for the last few years has been for this moment."

Ashlee blurted out, "I still don't understand what the problem is."

"I just keep thinking what if I don't get it? What am I supposed to do next?"

Ashlee responds, "Girl, stop! Stop thinking like that. You're going to mess around and manifest a negative outcome. You know your skill set, you know how hard you've been working, and you know where your heart is. It will work out, but you have to chill with the negative self-talk." Startled by Ashlee's lecture, Desirae uncertainly replied, "You're right, I know. It's just so easy to let my worries get the best of me."

"I've told you to try meditating or something. You have been so stressed lately and need to spend more time recharging."

Jennifer inserted, "I agree." She turned and placed the finished Rice Crispy treats into the refrigerator.

"I've heard you loud and clear this time. I will consider it," Desirae stated before gulping her wine. "And if that wasn't enough for the week, David dropped my ass by giving me an ultimatum to commit to a relationship, or he was done."

Ashlee let out a deep sigh, signaling her annoyance with Desirae's statement.

Jennifer responds, "Let her tell the story."

"According to him, he wants to love me, and I'm just this cold-hearted person that won't let him get close."

"Well, Desi, did you let him get close? And no, I'm not trying to be a bitch right now. I'm being your friend." Ashlee placed her hand on Desirae's arm. "I think this can be an opportunity to do some soul searching. Here is a man that has so many of the things you say you want that pretty much worships the ground you walk on, but you're running when things get too serious. Help me understand."

Shrugging her shoulders, she replied, "I don't know. It's hard to explain. I really do like him, and he treats me well, but I just don't have a desire to be in a relationship right now. I'm okay having casual situations, I'm just too busy for that."

Ashlee quickly countered, "Bullshit! I'm going to go ahead and call it what it is."

Desirae rolled her eyes as she took a sip of her wine. "You cannot tell me how the hell I feel."

"Sis, you're thirty. You keep this up you going to be the old lady with nine fucking cats." Jennifer pulled the Rice Crispy treats from the refrigerator and interjected, "This is about to go left, and we can't have that, so let me shut this down." She made eye contact with both women but rested on Desirae. "Des, what Ashlee is trying to say is that you are beautiful and have a lot going for yourself. You are a catch! But if you don't figure out what is driving this fear of connecting with a person outside of your comfort zone...you are going to miss out on something great one day. David might not be the guy for you, but you never going to find the right one as long as you keep moving this way."

Ashlee threw her hands in the air and added, "Right! Momma Jenn said what I was trying to say. But I want you to understand that I get so passionate about it because I see you let a great guy like David walk away but you have time for Malik ass."

Jennifer asked, "Well, Des? Why Malik?"

"I mean I understand that there will never be a romance story for us, and that is not something that I want either. And I know that spending too much time with him will only end badly, but the short time we're together just feels good. It's the perfect antidote for me right now."

Jennifer responded, "But all y'all do is have sex. There's nothing more to it."

"And maybe that's why it works for us. It's no pressure. The sexual chemistry has been unmatched by other guys. I'm not an idiot. I know Malik's interest doesn't reach beyond my body. But Malik doesn't press me to be something else or more to him. And I like that!"

Jennifer picked up the tray of snacks, turned the television to a movie, and ushered everyone to the living room. "Well, let's leave that subject alone. It's your life, and you'll eventually reach a point where you want more substance to your relationships. No one can force that on you. It has to be your decision."

The ladies walked over to the sofas, all finding a spot to settle in while eating their traditional homemade Rice Crispy treats and watching classic movies for the night.

CHAPTER 6

HOLES

8 Mile

Shortly after the plane landed, Desirae grabbed her carry-on luggage and exited. She had managed to catch a red-eye to meet with a client and return to Atlanta in the early afternoon. She noticed a bar in the concourse and stopped to debrief. After waiting impatiently, she seated herself in the corner near a wall filled with bottles of aging wine.

Eventually, a waitress came over and said, "Hello, ma'am, may I take your order?"

Desirae replied, "I'll have a vodka spritzer, please."

"Yes, ma'am. A strawberry martini coming right up."

"No, I asked for a vodka spritzer."

The waitress was noticeably distracted by her cellphone amidst the rendering of less than stellar service.

While waiting, Desirae reflected upon her career and her life. Reminiscing over unforgettable moments caused her to simultaneously experience nostalgia and grief. And by the time the waitress returned with her drink, she was too deep in thought to notice. She did, however, notice a gentleman standing at the hostess stand waiting to be helped.

She stood up and began to walk toward him. "I know this is not who I think it is," she said as she placed her hands on her hips. "Michael Evanston? Is that you?"

The gentleman turned around to look at Desirae and said, "Well now, that depends on who's asking."

"Desirae Sanders is asking, that's who."

He regarded her, the grin under his meticulously trimmed mustache playing second fiddle to the sparkle in his deep brown eyes. Michael Evanston looked to be a character from a soap opera, not like the dogged attorney that he had become over the years. The personification of tall, dark, and handsome, he was a mix between Michael B. Jordan and Regé-Jean Page. As a partner of the sister firm that Desirae worked for, he was well aware of her current disposition. There was hardly anyone in their circle who wasn't aware.

"Why don't you join me at my table?" Desirae offered. "You might be standing here for a while waiting on that waitress standing over there to seat you."

"You mean I get to have the honor of sitting with the Desirae Sanders? How did I get so lucky?"

"I'm not sure; let's just say that today is your lucky day," Desirae teased.

When they were seated, the waitress made her way back over to the table to inquire about Michael's order. "Is there something that I can get you?"

"I'll just have hot tea please."

"Hot tea?" Desirae exclaimed.

Michael nodded in confirmation to the waitress.

"Listen, you might be having tea, but right now, I need something a bit stronger."

Michael reached out to gently touch Desirae's hand. "Before you even say anything, please allow me to speak first. I know that your mind is racing a thousand miles per minute. The fact of the matter is that you earned your tenure as a partner of that firm a long time ago. And everyone who was anyone knew damn well that you deserved it."

Desirae turned to Michael in fury and asked, "Well, why the hell am I sitting here with my future in such a gray area huh?" She sat in silence for what felt like an eternity, and Michael allowed her to sit with the emotion.

He was conscious in a way that she hadn't known to be the norm. Eventually, he placed his hand on her shoulder cautiously and said, "Desirae, who are you?"

With a look of confusion, she replied, "So you want me to answer that? I mean what is this, an interview or something?"

Amused by her sarcasm, he retorted, "I'm serious. Who are you?"

"Well. I'm a woman who knows what she wants. I'm a lifelong learner, and I've built a career rooted in my love for the law. I like old school music, and a little trap music here and there if I'm with my girls and..."

Michael cut her off. "No Desirae, that's not what I'm asking. When you remove all of those things, who are you as a woman?"

Desirae had no words to give. She didn't know if she should be offended or turned on by his last statement. "Any man can see how beautiful you are and that you're brilliant and dedicated to your career. But I know that there's more to you than that."

Desirae gave Michael a smirk, definitely intrigued to get to know more about him. "How long have you been practicing that?"

"Hahaha. I haven't practiced anything. Now I would be lying if I said I never found you attractive or that I wanted to shoot my shot before. But timing is everything."

"True. And what are the chances of us being here together?"

"Exactly. So what's the answer to my question? I'd love to sit with you while you figure it out."

"Are you sure you have that much time?"

"To be frank, Desirae, I've got all the time you need."

And with a simple phrase, Desirae sat with Michael amidst conversation, food, and hot tea while discovering the strength to be vulnerable. They conversed until the sun went down and Michael offered to walk Desirae to her car. She declined when she discovered that they were parked at two different concourses, but reassured him that they could continue their discussion at any time. Their hug in parting was a little longer and a little closer than cohorts, further confirming that the deep conversation was a catalyst for more than a friendship.

Method Man

Pushing Jennifer's feet to the side, Derek declared, "I'll be back shortly. I need to run a quick errand."

"What errand do you have to run at 7 p.m.?"

"Well—" Derek paused.

"Well, what?" Jennifer inquired with her hands motioning for his response.

Derek sat up toward the edge of the sofa. "Can I be honest with you Jennifer, and you not get upset with me?"

"You already know you can tell me anything. What is it? You've got me worried now."

"The truth is that I just need to get out for a bit, baby. I need to drive with the windows down in the truck and feel the wind on my face. I can't get the image of you crying on that bathroom floor out of my head. My mind has been racing a thousand miles a minute since that moment. I worry about whether or not I'm able to be who and what you need right now." Derek placed his head in his hands and waited until Jennifer came and stood in front of him, placing his arms around her waist.

"You listen to me, Mr. McKinley. You're all I need to get by."

"Oh, you want to recite lyrics from Method Man right now, do you?"

They laughed together and held each other. "Now you go on out for your little joy ride or whatever you plan to do and bring yourself right back here to me, because I'll be right here, waiting on my man."

Derek scratched his head. "I don't deserve you, woman."

"You don't, but I'm yours anyway." Jennifer sat back down, and Derek kissed her on the forehead before grabbing his jacket and walking to the garage. With his hand on the door handle, he heard Jennifer's voice.

"Wait a damn minute."

Concerned, Derek turned around, and Jennifer was standing just behind him.

"Aren't you forgetting something?"

"Forgetting something?"

"You forgot to kiss me goodbye. I know you ain't about that life."

"My bad, Queen. I love you." Derek kissed Jennifer on the cheek and left through the garage door.

Derek got in the truck, turned on the engine, rolled down the windows, and checked his phone. There was an unanswered series of text messages, to which he replied, *Be there in 20*.

He drove for approximately 35 minutes until he reached a sign that read *Atlas*. He pulled to the back of the parking lot, placed the truck in park, and pulled out his phone to text.

I thought you said this place was private.

He received an immediate response: *Don't worry. No one you know is here. Valet and come inside. I'm standing near the bathrooms.*

Derek followed the direction and pulled around to the front of the building, where he was greeted by the attendant. As he entered, he recognized that the venue was a popular restaurant in Midtown.

"Shit. Shit. Shit," he squealed to himself. Another notification came through on his phone amidst his consternation. He noticed the sign for the restrooms and walked toward it.

"You promised me this night, Derek," said a voice from behind him.

"What the fuck. Why did you pick this place?"

"That's not what you should be worried about. It's cool here. What you should be worried about is the way you've been putting me on hold. I can't see you when I want to. I can't talk to you when I want to. And frankly, I'm tired of the bullshit."

"Shut the fuck up." Derek grabbed her by the neck and pushed her into the men's restroom. They kissed violently, and he pinned her against the wall of one of the bathroom stalls and ripped off her panties. He moved his hand from her neck up over her mouth, hoisted her up with his arms, and thrust inside of her. She bit his hand, adding to the tension of the moment. He continued to vigorously push inside of her until he heard footsteps and stopped.

She moaned, "Don't stop, baby. I don't care who knows."

"Bitch, shut up." They stood in silence, Derek still inside of her until the sound of the flushing toilet and footsteps leaving the restroom faded. Derek eased her down from against the stall wall and began to shake his head. "I can't do this shit, man. I love my wife, and this is all fucked up. I shouldn't even be here and neither should you." He pulled his pants back up, fastened his belt buckle, and left her to find her way out.

He drove the 35 minutes back home to find Jennifer on the couch in the same place they had been sitting before. As he walked past the living room, he heard Jennifer's voice faintly speak.

"Did you find what you were looking for, baby?"

"What I was looking for was here all along, baby. You're all I need to get by."

"Hush up, boy. I'll meet you in bed. Let's cuddle ourselves to sleep."

"That's exactly what I need, baby. Meet you there." Derek made his way to their bathroom and stood before himself in the mirror. He held his head in shame before turning on the shower to wash away the scent of his indiscretions before retiring to the bed that he shared with his wife.

Palais de Justice

Late that afternoon, Desirae sat behind the counsel's table until the courtroom was almost empty. The silence in the room was shattering. The only other person in the room besides the bailiff was the opposing counsel, who came by and placed his hand atop her shoulder before exiting the courtroom, which wasn't traditional practice, but the moment called for an act of humanness.

By the time she stood up, she was too numb to feel the walk of shame out of the courtroom. Her trek from the courthouse to her car was a blur. She sat in her car for over an hour in a trance before noticing a parking ticket atop her windshield, further confirming the storms raging at the moment. Eventually, her soul gave way to tears.

What had it all been for? All of the sleepless nights, the studying and preparation, the countless hours of group projects, the student loans, and the energy exerted to overcome self-doubt felt as though it was all for naught. How would she ever be considered for partner with such an excruciating loss on her record?

The notifications were the only thing that stopped her from cranking up the car and driving it straight into the oncoming traffic ahead. By the time she reached for her phone from the passenger's seat, she could see that all of the messages had been from Malik. Not one of her colleagues had texted to see how she was doing. News of verdicts in cases of this magnitude traveled faster than gossip, and she knew it.

It had been weeks since she'd returned from her visit to see him. He had not called or texted to even see if she'd arrived back at home safely. Resting her head on the steering wheel, she screamed in agony. "How stupid can I be?" she yelled out.

The pain in her soul was expressed more profoundly in her silence. What she most needed from Malik was love, but she hadn't asked it of him or herself. Instead, she'd settled for lust. And in her most vulnerable and trying moment, she found herself alone, a theme that was seemingly proving to be the story of her life. And amidst it all, she wrestled with the notion of texting him back because it was what she knew how to do.

Before she could make a decision, she was interrupted by a knock on her window. She looked up to see Latoya Ramirez, a high-powered attorney in Atlanta and everything Desirae aspired to become.

Desirae gathered her thoughts and got out of the car, secretly nervous to know what Latoya wanted.

"Hi, I'm Latoya Ramirez."

"Yes, ma'am, I know exactly who you are."

Latoya smiled in response to Desirae's eagerness in responding. "I saw what happened in the courtroom, and I've been following your career for a while now."

Desirae lit up from pure joy that she was even on Latoya's radar.

"What do you want your legacy to be?" she continued. Desirae found herself puzzled by the question and unable to answer, as it was something she had never thought about before. "Well, let's try this. Take a few days to think about that question, and once you know, give me a call." Latoya pulled her business card from her purse and handed it to Desirae. "Do not let what happened in there defeat you.

If you want more for your career, let's talk more. I see so much potential in you." Latoya gave a final small wave and walked away, reentering the courtroom.

Astounded by what had happened, Desirae found herself doing a small victory dance in the parking lot.

You Saw the Best in Me

In a mom-and-pop bistro, Ashlee found herself amidst routine. She stepped up to the coffee counter and said, "Morning. I'll have the usual please."

"One medium-hot almond milk matcha latte coming right up. Do you want the whipped cream on top with a dash of nutmeg today too, ma'am?"

"You got it. Damn, I guess I am here a lot."

"Well, we wouldn't have it any other way." The barista, a coy teenage boy, slender in stature with an overpowering purple gummy smile, managed to get Ashlee's attention and a solid tip for his attentiveness. To pass time, Ashlee strolled through her dating profile pondering whether she wanted to continue to use it after dating Tai didn't work out.

As Ashlee retrieved her drink, she noticed a familiar face entering the bistro. Her eyes widened, and she blurted out, "Cynt, is that you? Damn girl, of all the people that I run into, it's you?"

With a look of disappointment, Cynthia replied, "Well, would you like it to be someone else?"

Now stumbling over her words, Ashlee replied, "No. No. That didn't come out right. I'm just caught off guard. I mean, when I come here, I never see anyone I know, let alone someone with whom I've shared so much history with. This is like the place that I'm least likely to see a familiar face in Atlanta."

With a look of confusion on her face, Cynthia said, "Well. Okay. It was really good to see you. I hope you're doing well. I'd better get going."

Although it was an awkward moment, Ashlee pleaded, "Wait. Wait, is it...I mean would it be possible for you to sit with me for a second? I mean, I don't want to hold you up, I just..." She paused.

"You just what?"

Pissed, she exclaimed, "Damn it. This is more difficult than I imagined. Truth is, I wondered, hell even rehearsed what I would say and how I would act if I ever saw you again. And right now, at this moment, all that shit went out the window. I'm at a loss for words, but what I do know is that I just miss you. I've missed you since our last days together in college. And I haven't been able to get you out of my mind." Ashlee reached for her hand, and the touch sparked a resurrection of the history they'd once shared together. "Please, just sit with me for a moment if you can."

Still skeptical, Cynthia hesitated. "Only for a moment."

"This is about to sound crazy, but here goes nothing. I don't know where you live, who you are with, or what you do, and I don't care. I need you back in my life. It is not a coincidence that you are here. I tried to love every way possible and nothing has ever compared to what I've shared with you. Would you just...I mean could you just...SHIT. Is it possible that you would let me back in your life?" The silence was deafening. "Here's the thing. We've got way too much history to let love like this slip through our hands again. And let me be clear, if I can't have you the way I did before, then I don't want this at all."

Cynthia spoke carefully, "So you're saying that it's all or nothing for you?"

"That's exactly what I'm saying. Life is too short, man. And I'm not about that dating life. I thought I was, but I'm no good at it, it's not for me. I'm at a point in my life where either I settle down, or I don't." Leaning back in her seat, Ashlee proclaimed, "My life is good right now. I finally gave up all the shit from the past that weighed me down and ain't no way in hell I'm picking it back up. The only way I'm willing to risk my happiness is with you."

Cynthia, dazed by Ashlee's words, finally broke her silence. "I mean, I knew that you felt strongly for me in the past, but I'm not so sure that we should give this a second chance. After everything transpired the way that it had before we graduated from college, does this...us...does this really make sense?"

Ashlee leaned in to express herself more intently. "Would you let me tell you a story?"

"Sure." Cynthia shrugged her shoulders.

"There was a girl in her adolescent years who loved to play basketball and sports in general. She found that sometimes hanging with the guys was a little less complicated than hanging out with the girls. She even landed a job at the gym in her hometown because of how frequently she was there. One evening as she was cleaning up with one of her co-workers, he called her into the backroom to help him put away the towels. She was standing next to him when he attempted to kiss her. She pushed him away to show that she was not interested, but he forced her head toward his, making her kiss him. He threatened that if she did not do what he said, he would tell everyone that he knew she was gay. And that night, she laid there in silence with tears streaming down her face while he had his way with her. She never told a soul, and she never went back to the gym."

Catching on to Ashlee's story, Cynthia took hold of her hand. "You don't have to say anything more if you don't want to. I know that the story is about you. I can't begin to understand how hard this must have been."

Ashlee, now peering into the distance, continues. "There are days when working with my male clients proves to be challenging because I am often alone when working for them. That's why I always text either Desirae or Jennifer when I go to work, and of course, my dad knows where I am." With tears in her eyes, Ashlee went on softly. "I just feel like I'm always on guard because I never want to experience anything like that again."

"I had no idea that you had been through such a traumatic experience, Ashlee. Why didn't you share this with me when we were together before?"

"I really didn't know how to tell you. At the time, I was ashamed. I was also ashamed to admit that I was going to counseling to deal with it all, and all of my emotions. I can say that I am better because of therapy. I even started to write as a way of healing. I want to show you something." Ashlee pulled out a notebook filled with pages and pages of affirmations. She thumbed through them, allowing Cynthia to see before handing her the entire book. "I've never shown this to anyone. Hell, I've never even mentioned it to anyone, not even Desirae and Jennifer."

"So I'm the first person that you are sharing this with? Wow, this is really beautiful, Ash." As she took time to read a few of the affirmations, she looked back up at Ashlee with the book in her hands. "This. It's this that made me fall in love with you when we were in school. It was because you knew how to take lemons and turn them into lemonade. I don't think I've ever met someone who could make ugly things beautiful the way that you can. This is what my heart still yearns for."

Ashlee reached across the table and took ahold of Cynthia's hand. "Let's give us another try."

"I will agree, only if you must promise to be the truest version of yourself to the rest of the world. No more hiding. No more closeted existences. If you can agree to that, then I can agree to give us another chance."

"Done and done."

They both smirked before sealing their agreement with a kiss.

"And since we're making this official, I can tell you that I think you should take that book of affirmations and turn them into cards that everyone can use. I can't think of any person who doesn't need to be affirmed. I even know a company that can help you to get this done."

Ashlee turned to Cynthia and said, "Oh, that's what's up. I can even add some more things that are tailored toward healing. I would call them."

"I love it all," Cynthia said with a soft tone.

CHAPTER 7

KNOBS

The Irony

As the sun broke through the window of Desirae's bedroom, she was fighting to remain asleep in Michael's arms. Their love, now much stronger than she'd imagined, had been leading them to spend every free moment together, including sleeping hours.

Desirae crept out of the bed quietly, attempting to not wake him. She found herself standing in front of the bathroom mirror in one of Michael's large T-shirts washing her face. As she leaned over the sink to rinse her face, she felt Michael's hands lifting up the T-shirt and gliding between her legs. She stood back up with a smirk on her face while looking at him in the mirror. Michael began to kiss her neck while sliding his fingers across her pussy.

Desirae closed her eyes while laying her head back on his chest. She let out a soft moan while biting her lips. Michael was becoming more and more aroused by watching her responses to his touch. He whispered in her ear, "Whose is it?"

Desirae opened her eyes and made eye contact with Michael. "It's yours."

Michael slid his hands around her waist and up to her breasts, gripping them intensely while pressing up against her so that she could feel the stiffness of his dick.

Michael turned Desirae around to face him. She lifted her arms up as he pulled his shirt over her head, leaving her vulnerable to him in the most physical way but also ready to be taken by him. Michael kissed her passionately while hugging her, taking the time to give every curve of her body the attention that it deserved. As his hands reached her ass, he cupped it while biting her lip at the same time. Desirae looked into his eyes and smirked with excitement. It was these moments that she enjoyed so much. The intense sexual experience allowed her to feel free and intensively satisfied. Although Michael did not know the depths of her, he had mastered the ability to touch her soul sexually.

Still clutching her ass, Michael lifted her on top of the bathroom counter. Stepping forward, he slid the tip of his penis into her, enjoying the warm soft feeling of being stroked and hugged from all directions. Her soft moans and love face only intensified the experience for him. Michael loved to watch Desirae's responses to his movements; it was like a drug that drove him. Whether it was ego or adrenaline, Michael thrived from it.

As he continued to thrust in and out of Desirae, switching between fast and intense to a slow and gentle pace, she could see the sweat dripping down his muscular body frame that was complemented by hard, defined abs.

Michael had one hand wrapped around her thigh and the other around her neck. He gripped her neck with just the right strength to avoid interrupting air circulation but further her arousal. There was no question that Desirae was enjoying every second by the way her vagina was becoming wetter. Looking into her eyes, Michael instructed her to tell him how it felt. Desirae followed his instructions and began to describe how good it felt. As she was finishing her statement, he spit on her, ensuring it landed on her face. In response, Desirae opened her legs wider to give him even more control.

After a few more strokes, Michael stepped back and stared at Desirae, signaling with his hands for her to turn around. She slid off the sink counter and leaned against it, allowing Michael to push himself inside her from a different angle. He rested his hands on her waist as he thrust in and out of her, enjoying the friction. Michael watched her love face while stealing glances of her ass bumping up against him. As he felt the climax coming, Michael leaned forward against her, awaiting the feeling of release. Michael let out a loud groan as he deposited his seed into Desirae. Both become frozen as they attempted to catch their breath and reclaim normalcy after their escapade.

After a few moments passed, Michael grabbed a washcloth and began to clean up while Desirae went back to washing her face. Michael inquired about what Desiree had planned for the day.

"I was actually thinking we could get out and go to this new art museum that's opening."

"Whatever you want to do is cool with me."

"Okay, you don't have to get too dressed up. It's not anything fancy."

"I'll grab a few items from my place, and I'll be back in an hour or so. You want me to grab breakfast while I'm out?"

"No, let me cook you something," Desirae proclaimed as they both walked into the bedroom.

"Well now, I could get used to this."

"Yeah, well maybe we'll get to a point where no one will have to leave to get their clothes."

Michael stopped in his tracks. "Are you saying what I think you're saying?"

"I'm saying that we are spending so much time together, it only makes sense that we at least place the discussion of living together and the future on the table."

"Wow." Michael stood in silence.

Noticeably bothered, she said, "Uh, are we not on the same page here because I'm feeling kind of crazy right now. Don't leave me out here on this island by myself, Michael."

Perplexed, he responded, "No. No. Um. Sorry, baby, that's not it. I just can't believe we're here already. I mean time has flown by, and I had no idea we were progressing so fast."

Agitated, Desirae stood up to address Michael eye to eye. "Well, weren't you the one who said that I was your peace? Who the hell says that to someone if they aren't ready for long term commitment? Listen, Michael, I don't have time to waste. All of my time is valuable as is yours. And if we aren't going anywhere with this, we can just end it all here. Life is way too short."

"You're blowing this way out of proportion. You're taking this way too far, and you're missing what I'm saying."

"Well, what are you saying Michael? Because it sounds like you are unsure of whether or not you want a future with me."

"Stop, Desiboo! Whatever is happening right now is not about me or us. Let's talk, and I need you to hear me." Michael grabbed Desirae's hands and guided her to the foot of the bed. "What I am saying is that I agree with you, life is short and we both deserve to know as much as possible about each other before committing to a life of love together. I never once said I didn't want that with you."

Desirae interjected, "But—"

"But nothing. There has been no conversation before to let me know that you changed the rules. We have had several conversations about your past, so the last thing I want to do is rush you."

"You're right," Desirae ashamedly admitted.

"So I'm going to get a few things from my place while you cook breakfast. When I get back, we will talk about what our future looks like together, but that fear in you is not going to drive me away. I got you, I got us." Michael stood to grab his wallet and keys from the dresser, stopping to kiss Desirae on her forehead before exiting.

Once Desirae heard the door close, she flopped back on the bed and uttered the words...THIS IS A REAL MAN... I THINK I'M IN LOVE.

Expecting

"Wait, baby. Wait. Before we go inside, I just want to say that I know today is a big day. We've spent hours on end talking about building our legacy together. Most importantly, I just want you to know that no matter what happens in this building, we are in this together." Derek sealed his heartfelt words with a kiss atop Jennifer's forehead.

She replied with raised eyebrows, "Til death do us part?"

"Till death do us part, baby," he repeated while opening the door for her to enter. Once inside, Jennifer walked toward the receptionist desk to check in, and Derek located two seats in the middle of the room near a small aquarium.

As he sat down, he took a big breath and exhaled with his eyes closed. Unbeknownst to Jennifer, Derek too felt the weight of the moment, although he knew better than to let Jennifer know his true sentiments. By the time she sat down, she was aggressively biting her lower lip, which confirmed that her nerves had gotten the best of her. Her thoughts were interrupted with a text from Desirae informing her that she had decided to leave her firm and work with her newfound mentor. But before Jennifer could gather the words to congratulate her on her big decision, her name was called again to verify her identity and insurance information.

Now seated again, Derek grabbed ahold of Jennifer's hand and kissed her gently on the cheek. "Derek, even I'm honestly not sure about all of this. I mean, is this necessary? We're preparing to make a huge investment in something that will probably happen for us on our own if we just have a little more patience and a little more faith."

Before Derek could answer, a short, stout nurse with wiry salt and pepper hair and heavy black eyeliner was standing before them to escort them through the double doors into the doctor's quarters. Although she didn't appear to be friendly at first, her voice and demeanor told a completely different story.

Walking at a fast pace down the hallway while escorting them through the corridor, she said, "Mr. and Mrs. McKinley. I'd like to begin by welcoming you into our office. Everyone around here becomes family, and I promise that we will do everything in our power to take very good care of you. I've been working here and serving families just like yours for over 20 years, and believe me when I say it has been a blessing to me to be a blessing to others. Now before we get started, I'll be taking a few vitals for each of you right here in Room 3. Afterward, we will have you meet with the doctor for your complete consultation and review of the process from start to finish."

Jennifer and Derek sat closely nestled both amidst their own thoughts and observations of the space, not knowing what to expect.

"Mr. McKinley, I'll have you step up first. Let's get your weight and blood pressure. Mrs. McKinley, let's place this on your pointer finger and rest it right on your knee so that we can check your oxygen levels, and then I'll have you switch."

While working them through the preliminary process, the nurse seemed to find the words of comfort they both needed to hear. "Making the decision to start your family is one that will bless your lives forever. Believe me, babies are God's gift to those that love each other, and I can tell that you two sure do love each other. I love to see it. Now let's get you all finished up and in with Dr. McCloud." She escorted them into the doctor's office and bid them adieu. Just before closing the door, she peeked her head back in and said, "Remember, everything will work out just like God planned for you. Remember that." She winked her eye and smiled and disappeared behind the door.

Derek and Jennifer sat in silence for a hint of eternity, wondering about what would happen next and what the doctor might say. Jennifer's weight felt more like guilt as she felt responsible for them being there. Trying desperately to not succumb to the thickness of the air, she could no longer hold back the tears. She turned her body slightly in an attempt to hide her sorrow from Derek, who appeared to be grappling with his own series of thoughts. By the time the silent tension in the room climaxed, there was a firm knock on the door and a voice emerged.

A lanky, towering figure with dark features, a firm face, and a deep voice greeted them with an extended hand. "Mr. and Mrs. McKinley, my name is Dr. McCloud. It's a pleasure to meet you. I'm going to assume that you are here to talk about making babies and not just to take me out to lunch," he said with a hearty laugh.

Derek and Jennifer looked at one another and burst into laughter. The doctor was a clear pro at easing the tension in the air with what he thought to be a comedy. "No. No sir. Not lunch today, but if we can manage to get ourselves pregnant with your help, then we will be more than happy to do the honors," Derek replied in kind.

"And that we shall do. I'm telling you now that Ruth's Chris is my favorite, so get your money ready. I'm not a cheap date." Laughing once more and redirecting the conversation, he said, "Now let's get down to business. After reviewing your charts and questionnaires, I understand that you desire to take a very aggressive approach to this process, and I assure you that we will do everything in our power to be of service. And while this process is not 100 percent, our fertilization rate is one that our practice is most certainly proud of. I'd like to start by sharing with you that this will be a journey, and one that I'm sure you know is more of a marathon than a sprint. I'd like to say that it's a perfect process, but nothing could be further from the truth. Yet and still, we realize miracles every day, and we hope that one of those miracles has your name on it. Let us begin by having you each share a little about your desire to have a family with me. I find that when couples express their wants, needs, and desires about starting a family together, we all learn a great deal about the power of making plans for ourselves in accordance with what God has planned for us. Mrs. McKinley, I'd like for you to go first."

Jennifer began to pour out her heart to Derek and the doctor, disclosing the abortion she'd had as a teenager and her fear that her current struggles were a result of it. Derek sat in awe of the woman that he'd married, recognizing her strength and that he was certain that he had chosen who he wanted to be with for the rest of his life come hell or high water. Caught up in the rapture of their deepest desire, Jennifer and Derek left all of their outward expressions about their quest to join together to bring about new life in the doctor's office and silently summoned the heavens to make it all come true.

Too Hot to Hold

Very rare did Ashlee find herself with a free day of no work or parenting duties. Days had passed, and every idle moment was filled with thoughts of Cynthia. Notifications on her phone generated anxiety and hope that it would be her. Becoming more restless by the minute, Ashlee decided to break the boredom with sexual pleasure. She grabbed a small T-shirt from the chest and lay across the bed, placing it between her thighs and directly under her vagina. She closed her eyes, squeezed her thighs together, and began to drift away.

Ashlee walks into the kitchen to find Cynthia standing aside from the kitchen island in a button-down top and thigh length skirt. Cynthia is so focused on chopping vegetables that she does not hear Ashlee enter the room. Ashlee steps directly behind her, pressing her body against hers and moving her long tresses with her hand to expose her neck. Simultaneously, Ashlee begins to kiss on her neck and slide her free hand up Cynthia's skirt, not stopping until her fingertips meet her bare exposed pussy.

Ashlee whispers in her ear, "Lift your skirt and widen your legs if you want me to keep going." Cynthia, caught in the moment, fails to comply with Ashlee's request, which results in Ashlee removing her fingers. Cynthia lets out a frustrated "No!" to which Ashlee responds with, "Then follow my instructions."

Cynthia quickly takes a step to place more space between her legs and lifts her skirt up. Ashlee takes her right hand and squeezes her petite but plump ass while gliding her tongue from the lower of Cynthia's neck to her ear. She pauses to demand, "Bend over and don't move until I tell you to."

In full submission, Cynthia bends over, allowing her upper body to become parallel to the kitchen island. Ashlee drops to her knees, and with both hands spreads Cynthia's cheeks, exposing both her ass and pussy. Captivated by both, Ashlee digs in, sliding her tongue from the clitoris to the ass. Noticing a slight shift in Cynthia's body language, Ashlee pleasures her ass by brushing her tongue repeatedly against the opening. As Cynthia lets out a soft moan, Ashlee spits to make things more slippery and applies pressure behind until her tongue has a slide inside of Cynthia.

Initially tightening up, Cynthia quickly settles from the pleasure of feeling Ashlee's tongue inside of her. Ashlee firmly instructs her to hold her ass open, which allows Ashlee to resume fucking her ass with her tongue and shifting her left hand down to her pussy. She massages her clitoris and surrounding area with her middle and ring fingers, gliding them back and forward *as the spit continues to flow down and gets her ass messier.*

Ready to make Cynthia climax, Ashlee slides her fingers inside of Cynthia's pussy while continuing to slurp and lick her ass. Witnessing ... thighs tightening, Ashlee employs faster and harder strokes, knowing that this will intensify the sensation for her. In an unwanted desire to run from what is coming, Cynthia spreads her legs more and stands on her toes, to which Ashlee follows in pursuit, digging her face in more and picking up the flow with her fingers. Encouraged by the squashing sound of her pussy, Ashlee does not let off until Cynthia lets out a loud final moan and her body ceases to shiver.

Just as Ashlee reached her climax in real life, she received a text from Cynthia. *Hey, what are your plans tonight? I want to see you.*

Oh nothing, going through ideas for new recipes. Come over, Nolan is gone for the weekend. Ashlee reflected on the thought of how crazy it was that they were so in sync with each other, shown by the fact that Cynthia had been thinking about her at the very moment that Ashlee's heart and body were craving her.

Okay, I'll be there in thirty minutes. I'm not far. Ashlee sat in silence, amazed at how Cynthia made her soul glow. Realizing that thirty minutes would fly by, Ashlee jumped up to clean the house quickly and shower. Although she'd known Cynthia forever, she still felt the desire to impress her.

Breadth

Two weeks after the gruesome trial, Desirae found herself pacing back and forth in her office until a knock at the door revealed Samantha's face. It was comforting as Samantha, her assistant for several years, was well aware of the outcome of the trial and that Desirae's chances at becoming a partner were likely to be dismissed. The look on Desirae's face was distraught.

Samantha spoke life. "I know that I am not seeing the strongest woman that I know allowing a moment like this to steal her thunder."

"That's just it, Sam. I'm tired of being the strong one. At what point does someone stand up for me? Shit!" she shrieked before spiraling. "In my life, I had to be strong for my brothers when my mother was out of her fucking mind. I had to be strong for my classmates, and at times I carried the load of the work in undergrad. I had to be strong for my damn self while working two jobs and attempting to get myself through law school. And when I got to this law firm, which I believed to be my dream job, I've had to be a servant to my cohorts in the firm as the only Black woman here, receiving no credit in return. Why the hell must I be strong all the time?"

"Now just hold on, Desirae. It's true. You've done so much for so many, and you are most deserving of the reward of being named partner and so much more."

"Well, where is it, Sam? Where is the reward you seem so sure of? I want to say fuck this shit and walk out of here. Why should I stick around for them to tell me that my work has been in vain? Fuck that! I've paid my dues. I should not be experiencing a moment like this." Desirae stood up again and transitioned to rage. "Fuck this shit," she exclaimed as she began to pack her belongings. "By the time they get around to telling me that I was not selected as a partner, I'll be far away. As a matter of fact, help me collect my personal items so that I never have to return to this place."

"Well now, there is the Desirae that I know. Do you have another plan in mind for what you're going to do next?" Sam inquired.

"There is potential somewhere else, but I have to look more into it."

Desirae and Samantha added as much as they could to their belongings so as to not give notice to the associates in preparation to exit the office. Upon leaving, Desirae said her normal goodbyes. "I hope that everyone has an amazing weekend. Great work this week, guys. Great work."

The associates waved goodbye as Desirae and Samantha walked to the parking garage. Once there, Samantha unloaded the items that she'd collected into Desirae's trunk while Desirae unloaded more items into the backseat of her car. Once done, Desirae plopped into her car, wrapped her arms around the steering wheel, and wept.

Samantha noticed Desirae's dismay and motioned for her to roll down the window. "Remember, anyone can quit, but only winners know how to hold it together when everything around them appears to be falling apart. You got this, so don't worry."

"I don't know what I would do without you, Sam, I really don't," Desirae stated as she reached her hand out of the window to grab ahold of Samantha's. They squeezed tightly, both recognizing that it was an agreement to move forward at all costs and by any means necessary.

CHAPTER 8

SOCKETS

Unraveled Reality

A month had passed since starting their fertility treatments. Both Jennifer and Derek often found themselves eager to know if the work they were doing would produce the child they so badly wanted. Small things like grocery shopping together had become the things that served as perfect distractions for the couple.

"I think that's everything we needed," Jennifer said while scanning the list for a final time. "Oh, no, I forgot my Twizzlers!"

Derek frowned in response to her statement. "I don't know how you eat them; they are tasteless."

"Whatever. Meet me at the front. I'm going to go get them."

"All right. I'm going to do one more sweep of the chip aisle first," Derek informed her. They parted ways, going in opposite directions. As Derek turned the corner, he was immediately met with a familiar face.

"Hey, Derek."

Startled, he responded, "Hey, Rebecca."

"I'm surprised to see you here," Rebecca said in a hesitant attempt to check Derek's temperature.

"Yeah, well, nice seeing you," Derek responded while attempting to scurry past her.

"Wait! I've been trying to reach you. You've been ignoring me."

"It's all good. I'm trying to take care of my family and what we had going is not conducive to that."

"So just like that, you're done with me?" Rebecca asked while fighting back tears.

Derek took a moment to check his surroundings, trying to ensure Jennifer had not returned to look for him. "Yes, it's over. I don't understand why you're making it a big deal. We were having fun, and you knew what it was all along."

"Did I know you had a wife at home? Absolutely. But I thought you cared about me too. At least enough to end things with me properly."

"Maybe I should have, but I'm doing it now. Just let it go and move on with your life. I am."

Tears started to run down Rebecca's face as she held her stomach with her free hand. Derek noticed the gesture and froze. The opportunity to inquire was quickly eliminated by the sound of Jennifer's voice as she turned the corner.

"Get your shit together, Jen is coming," Derek hissed in panic. "Hey, babe, this is Rebecca from the office. I believe you met her at the business banquet."

"Yes, I remember. Hi!" Jennifer joined the conversation while adding her things to the cart and stepping closer to Derek. She noticed that Rebecca had been crying by the color of her eyes, but avoided asking out of respect for privacy. "How have you been? It's been a while since the banquet."

"I'm well. Yes, it has been a while. You look great!"

"Aww, thanks. You look amazing yourself. That waistline!"

The two women shared a short laugh as Derek placed his arm around Jennifer, which sent chills through Rebecca.

"Are you still at the office?"

"Not anymore. My role there was on a short-term basis, so once they were done with me, I was out with the wind," Rebecca asserted while cutting her eyes at Derek.

"Derek, babe, I cannot believe y'all are that cold up there."

"Jenn, I am not HR, that is outside my arena."

Jennifer turned her attention back to Rebecca. "Well, I hope you were able to find something else. I hate that you were let go like that."

"Oh yes, I'm working at a firm downtown for now. So far it has the potential to turn into something long term."

"I'm so happy things worked out for you. Blessings on top of blessings."

"Yes, you are right," Rebecca responded while caressing her stomach.

Elevated by the news, Jennifer responded, "Oh my, congratulations!"

Feeling the walls crumbling quickly, Derek exited the situation by telling Jennifer that they should head toward the checkout lines.

"Okay, Derek. Well, Rebecca, I'm going to get your number from Derek. I remember him telling me that you're not from here so we should definitely grab lunch sometime."

"Thank you, you're so sweet." Rebecca turned and walked in the opposite direction, quickly going down an aisle.

Derek and Jennifer found themselves at the front of the store, waiting in line. "She is so nice. You should've introduced us a long time ago. I could've invited her out with the girls."

"Yeah, I won't be trying to bring work home. Plus, you know the three musketeers are real territorial."

Laughing, Jennifer responded, "No, we're not! But she seems cool. I'm sure Des and Ashlee would like her."

"Okay, if you say so," Derek responded timidly.

Derek received a text message notification on his phone. A part of him was terrified to read it because he knew it was probably from Rebecca. Thoughts were racing through his mind. Was she pregnant or faking it to rattle him? If she was pregnant, could it be his? Was her crazy ass really about to befriend his wife? With the swipe of a finger, Derek's fate was revealed.

Yes, the baby is yours!

No Turning Back

"Look, Mommy! Look how high I can go!" Nolan screamed out as he aimed to swing higher and higher. Ashlee broke from her nervous thoughts to acknowledge Nolan's eagerness to show her his accomplishment. "Yes, baby, I see." She turned to find Xavier laughing at her. "What is so funny?"

"You! Why are you so nervous?"

"Umm, this is a big deal!" Ashlee's thoughts were racing over the idea of Cynthia meeting Nolan for the first time. Not only that, but this would be her first time introducing Nolan to his mom dating women.

"Of course, it's a big step. But everything will be all right. You believe Cynt is good for you and will be good for Nolan?"

"Yes, she's amazing. You will like her."

"Okay, well, chill and let everything flow."

"Okay, okay. You're right. But do you think it's too early to tell him about my sexuality?"

"Honestly, that is up to you. But if you're not going to tell him, don't do it out of fear."

Ashlee nodded to show that she agreed with his advice.

Minutes passed as the two followed Nolan around as he explored the park's playground. A tap on the shoulder brought Desirae to this pivotal moment that would collide her two worlds.

"Hey, babe." Ashlee turned to see Cynthia's glowing skin and beautiful smile. Simply catching a sniff of her dewy perfume made Ashlee's heart melt. Immediately noticing Ashlee's anxiousness, Cynthia whispered in Ashlee's ear, "It's going to be okay. You are showing your son what it looks like to live as your authentic self. Don't overthink it, just let things flow organically."

"Hey, I'm Xavier." He stepped toward the couple with his hand out.

"Hi, I'm Cynthia!" she responded while moving past the hand gesture and going for a hug. "I'm sorry, but I'm a hugger and you'll get used to it."

"Oh okay, you plan on sticking around for a while?"

"Of course. I wouldn't be interested in the idea of meeting Nolan if I wasn't serious about what we're doing."

"Okay, Okay. I like that. So how do you feel about the parenting arrangement that Ash and I have?"

"Umm, I love it. I think it's great that Nolan gets to see his parents get along so well even though you're not together. I'm simply here to be an additional source of love and support for him."

Xavier smiled and looked at Ashlee. "You bet not fuck this up. She's a keeper."

"Aww shut up," Ashlee yelled while playfully pushing Xavier.

The trio continued to have short conversations until Nolan came rushing at them full speed. "Mommy, Mommy. Can I have some ice cream?" He pointed at the ice cream truck parked nearby.

Danielle Latrice

"Sure, let's all have some ice cream." They turned and started to make their way to the other end of the park. "Baby, I want you to meet Mommy's friend Ms. Cynthia."

"Hi, Ms. Cynthia!"

"Hi, Nolan."

"So you're Mommy's friend?"

"Yes, I am."

"I have a friend named Dylan. He's my best friend. We like to play Fortnite together."

"Oh really? You'll have to show me how to play one day."

"I can show you. My dad is really good, though. It's hard to beat him."

"I'll have to get really good then."

"Yep. Really good."

Ashlee was watching the two interact and finding herself falling more and more in love with Cynthia by the second. "Nolan, it looks like the truck is about to leave."

"No! Let's run, Ms. Cynthia."

"Okay!" They both took off toward the truck, leaving Xavier and Ashlee behind.

"So what do you think?"

"Honestly, Ash, so far so good. You know Nolan is a friendly child anyway, so I don't know why you were worried about it going left."

"That's true."

Xavier received a phone call from Vicky, which he stepped away to take. As Ashlee got closer to the truck, it became clear that the new besties were in their own world, already enjoying their popsicles.

"Mommy, here. I got you a pink one."

"Thanks, baby."

Nolan handed his mom her popsicle and then entered his own fantasy world, making rocket ship noises for his popsicle.

"Where's Xavier?" Cynthia asked with concern.

"He's over there on the phone with Vicky. I keep telling him that the relationship is not going to work. I would bet money that she is complaining right now about him being here with me."

"Well, does she know that your preference is women?"

"Yes, he has explained that to her, but she is not hearing it. In her eyes, he can be a great father without having to be around me as much as he is."

"Oh, wow. That is not the energy you want from the person you're dating when you already have a child."

"All facts! I've even volunteered to meet with the girl to help soothe things over, but she wasn't interested. But then he wonders why I have an issue with Nolan being around her."

Nolan, listening to the adult's talk, decided to add to the conversation. "Mommy, is Ms. Cynthia your friend like Auntie Ash and Auntie Des? If so, is she going to have sleepovers too?"

Ashlee and Cynthia shared startled looks with each other, clearly taken by surprise that he was even listening. "Umm, no baby. Ms. Cynthia is my friend like Ms. Vicky is your dad's friend."

"Oh, so two girls can like each other like that? Daddy and Ms. Vicky kissed."

"Yes, baby. There are people in the world that like each other regardless of if they are the same gender."

"And boy and girl are genders?"

"Yes, Nolan, that is right."

"Well can't you just change your gender and be a boy so you can be girl and boy together?"

Ashlee took a moment to collect her thoughts. She wanted to explain everything to Nolan, but she also did not want to confuse him due to his age and his inability to fully comprehend. "No, it doesn't work like that. But finish eating your ice cream. We can talk about it later."

"Okay!"

Ashlee received a text message notification from Cynthia: *You did well. Don't feel compelled to make him understand everything right now.*

Cynthia reached for Ashlee's hand to give her support. She was aware of how big of a deal this moment was for Ashlee, and she was so proud of her.

My Pleasure

Sitting in her car early in the morning before preparing for the day was Desirae's newfound version of self-care. As she exhaled, the vibrating phone disrupted the moment.

"Good morning, babe," she said, hurrying to finish her small breakfast.

"Good morning, beautiful. I had to be the first person that you spoke to this morning. It just had to be me."

"And how do you know that I haven't spoken to anyone else just yet?"

"Well, even if you have, they can't say the things that I can to you. I intend to speak to your soul, meanwhile, those other guys are still learning how to talk."

Even with all of her effort, Desirae was unable to hold back the grin that was now plastered across her face. It was actually moments like these that Desirae found herself amazed that she'd found someone that made her want to be vulnerable. Plus the sex was amazing.

"You're right, baby. You're different."

"Wow, I don't know how to take that."

"No, different in a good way. It's like you've made me feel again. It's been so long since I felt this way about someone, I believe I had convinced myself that it didn't exist in me anymore."

"Well let me be clear, I see you. Even when it's hard for you to see how amazing and beautiful you are, I see it. And every chance I get, I'm going to remind you of it."

"See that's what I'm saying, you're so freaking perfect! I probably would have never left the firm if it weren't for your love and support. I mean look at me, sitting here on the heels of a new moment in my career. I can honestly say that I am happy, and I could have never imagined I would discover happiness outside of the dream that I worked for over ten years to attain."

"And this is only the beginning for you. Babe, you are meant to do great things. You're stepping into your purpose, and I'm blessed to be able to witness it."

"Aww, thanks love."

"Well, I'm not going to hold you. Good luck on your first day. Call me when you leave. Love you."

"Love you too."

As Desirae disconnected the call, she looked in the rearview mirror and coiled her hair with her fingers. She reached in the console, retrieved a tube of nude lipstick, applied it to her lips, and hit the button to open the garage door. As she put on her seatbelt, she smiled to herself, experiencing the fullness of inner peace. Her drive to work was smooth and relaxing, allowing her to run through her favorite affirmations. As she pulled up to the building, her new place of practice, she was engulfed in laughter. With hope in her eyes and a will to win in her heart, she opened the door and was met with the smell of fresh ambition. She reached into the back seat to grab her leather briefcase and Prada blazer and put it on. The warm sun illuminating the rims of her oversized glasses was just the welcome she needed as she entered the building.

At the front entrance, she was greeted by a stubby, bald gentleman with dark features and bushy eyebrows wearing a navy blue pinstripe suit. His hand was extended as he neared her with a welcoming, sizable smile. "Desirae, we are all so happy that you are here. It's officially time to write a new chapter in your law career. Are you ready?"

"Good morning, Mr. Newberry. I'm so ready," she replied.

"Well then, let's build the career of your dreams, shall we?"

Desirae followed Mr. Newberry to the elevator to begin the day, now believing in her heart that she had managed to shatter the glass ceiling that she seemingly could not break through. The elevator stopped at the 10th floor, where a brown-skinned slender woman stepped on.

"Hi, Mr. Newberry. How is your morning?"

"Hi, Rebecca. It's busy as usual, but I wouldn't want it any other way." They shared a short laugh. "Let me not be rude. Desirae, this is Rebecca. Rebecca, this is Desirae. Rebecca is doing some consulting for us, but we're hoping she will return after the baby comes." Mr. Newberry gave Rebecca a warm smile.

"Yes, I hope to return as well. Desirae, you will love it here. Everyone is nice, and the firm is really big on investing in their employee's future."

"That sounds perfect. Congratulations also, you're glowing!" Desirae responded before following Mr. Newberry off the elevator.

An office assistant greeted her. "You can have a seat in here. Mrs. Ramirez is finishing a meeting and will be right in."

Desirae sat in silence while responding to Ashlee's and Jennifer's encouraging messages for her first day.

"Hi, I'm so sorry to keep you waiting," Mrs. Ramirez proclaimed while entering the room with so much charisma and high energy that it took over the room.

"It's no problem. I'm just taking in the beautiful view that you have."

"Yes, it's quite beautiful. If you don't mind, I would like to take this to the sofa. I want this to be a very relaxed conversation."

"Sure." Desirae relocated to the sofa, sitting just a few feet from Mrs. Ramirez. "I know we talked briefly over the phone when you accepted the opportunity to come work with me and become my mentee. I'm curious to know what led to you making the decision."

"Honestly, I had to do some real self-evaluating and after sitting with my thoughts I was able to own the fact that I'm not happy."

"Do you have an idea of why you're not happy?"

"I think the main reason is that I lost myself in my career journey. I graduated from law school with so many dreams and aspirations, but somewhere along the road, I convinced myself that there is no room for dreams. So I went with the most stable opportunity at the time and spent years trying to climb the ladder there."

"Well, what is it that you want?"

"I want to feel fulfilled in the work that I'm doing. I want to take cases that change lives. I want to actually do things that change the community around us."

Mrs. Ramirez sat in silence with a grin on her face. "I'm so proud that you did the work in that short time since speaking with you outside the courthouse. You looked so defeated that day, which is a complete change from who is sitting in front of me today. I cannot promise that the journey I am preparing to take you on will be easy, but I promise it will be worth it."

"I'm ready! I am here for a reason, and I am choosing to trust the process. It's time I fight for the future I want."

"That is what I like to hear. So let's get you started on an official tour of the place, and then you can get settled into your new office."

Refresher for the Soul

Time had flown by with the women enjoying their busy lives that had come to be filled with such bliss. To recharge, Desirae, Jennifer, and Ashlee found themselves enjoying a girl's night at a local trap and paint event. Discovering that their arrival was early, the girls took advantage of the reasonable music level and indulge in catching up to speed with each other's lives.

"So how are you and Michael? We only met him once, but things must be good that he's kept you away," Jennifer said to tease Desirae.

"We know everything is good because she's still infatuated with him. The only person that can keep your attention is Malik. So?" Ashlee added in.

Overtaken with joy, Desirae spoke through her grin. "Things are amazing! It's so crazy because months ago I wouldn't have imagined being here today feeling so in love and so connected to a man. He's so patient; even when I'm losing my shit, he becomes my calm."

"Okay, I'm loving this. What about Malik?" Jennifer inquired.

"Girl, Malik who? I let him go. I don't need him anymore. The closer Michael and I got, the less interested I became in what Malik and I had going."

"I'm here for it all. But how did Malik take the news that you were moving on?"

"Girl. He doesn't care. In his mind, he knows I'll be back and I'm not going to find what we have sexually with anyone else."

The girls sat in silence waiting to hear whether Malik's accusations were true to Desirae.

"And no, he's wrong. Michael's sex is great. I believe the fact that there is passion and intimacy involved changes everything."

Jennifer interjected, "I'm glad you got to this point. We knew you would one day."

The girls shared short cheers as a celebratory moment of Desirae's evolution in her love life.

"But what about y'all? What's tea?"

Excited to share her news, Ashlee quickly started talking. "Y'all already knew that I rekindled things with Cynt."

Desirae exclaimed, "Yes, I remember. The idea of y'all crossing paths is just crazy."

"I know, right? Well, things are great! She's met Nolan and Xavier already, who love her."

"Aww, that is so great! I am so happy for you. I know how important it was to you for Nolan to like her," Jennifer uttered.

"Yes. It could have been complicated, but it wasn't."

"So how much did you explain to Nolan?"

"That was the tricky part. I think a part of me is so excited to finally be at the point where I'm ready to live my truth, that I forgot that everyone is going to go at their own pace to accept and understand who I am. So, with Nolan, we explained that Cynthia was my friend like Vicky is to his dad. I briefly explained that girls can like girls. I didn't go beyond that."

Puzzled to know more, Desirae asked, "Well, do you think he understands?"

"Honestly, I don't know if he understands completely. Hell, I don't know if he even cares. I think what I told him is good for now, and I'll explain more if he comes to me with more questions or when he gets a little older."

Jennifer interrogated, "Okay, so what's next?"

"Cynt is going to meet my dad before the family reunion and then she's going to accompany me to the family reunion with Nolan."

Desirae inserted her two cents. "Well, we already know Pops is not going to care because he already knows about you. The real question is what is your mom going to do?"

Ashlee explained, "All facts. But I have to do this. Cynt has made it clear she's not going to be a secret or be a victim to my inability to live my truth this time, so I'm doing what I have to do."

Disturbed by Ashlee's response, Jennifer asked, "That sounds like her ass is not being sensitive to the position that you're in."

"Could she be more patient while I figure it out? Yes, but I can't tell her how to feel considering how I broke her heart last time. Plus, I know this is what I need to do."

Still, in disagreement, Jennifer sipped her glass of water and refrained from further commenting on the subject.

"Well, good luck, Ash. I'm sure things will work out fine," Desirae added to give Ashlee some form of reassurance.

Noticing that the crowd was starting to pile in, Desirae turned to Jennifer. "Ma'am, come on with the tea before we can't hear you."

Her radar was spot on because it became clear by the slight increase in volume that the DJ was gearing up.

"Well, mines are simple. Derek and I have started fertility treatment, and I'm quitting writing for good."

"Hold on, now, you're going to have to give us more backstory than that," Desirae proclaimed.

"The writing part is simple. I want to give everything to my family and our effort to have a child. I don't want this secret."

The girls did not respond to that statement, but that didn't surprise Jennifer, given that she was fully aware that they weren't in favor of her shrinking her writing life already. "And the fertility thing has been something I was struggling with for a while now. We went and got tested, and it was determined that I was going to need help."

"But why didn't you tell us you were dealing with that?"

"I didn't want to be a burden. I knew y'all had a lot on your plates already."

Frustrated by her answer, Desirae responded, "Absolutely not. That's not what we do. We are sisters, and we are supposed to hold each other up. You cannot be holding things like that back. I can only imagine how many times you needed to talk but chose to keep it bottled up inside."

"I mean, you're right. It's been a rough couple of months."

Ashlee piped in, "And where has Derek been during this time?"

"He was around, but he didn't know."

"How the hell he didn't know?"

"I didn't tell him. I was hiding from him too. I was honestly ashamed of it all and didn't know how to talk about it."

Placing her hand on Jennifer's leg, Ashlee replied, "There is nothing to be ashamed about at all. You are going to have these treatments and a beautiful baby. And we are going to be there for you going forward. Understood?"

"Yes, understand."

Desirae firmly lectured, "Don't you ever do something like that again!"

"I won't. I love y'all."

"We love you too."

And just on cue, the DJ started the event, overshadowing any attempt of a conversation the girls desired to have.

They finished the night out dancing, painting, and enjoying these fulfilling moments of sisterhood.

.

CHAPTER 9
EDGE

A Fork in The Road

Months had gone by since meeting Michael, and what seemed like the perfect ending to her years of inability to love again had taken an unexpected shift. Although they'd mutually decided to not move in together, they continued to spend every second they could in each other's presence. But for the last three weeks, Michael's behavior had become different—very moody and distant. What once was warm kisses and endless lovemaking had been replaced with dry hugs and empty kisses. In Desirae's mind, all she could think of was that he was cheating, which only made her further explore whether this was her karma for breaking so many men's hearts over the years.

Unable to take it anymore, Desirae decided to confront Michael when he came over to her house later that day. She had spent the entire evening cooking dinner for the two of them, something that she knew he usually enjoyed for her to do; but once again he displayed no interest in eating and sat quietly on the sofa.

"Look Michael, I think it's best if I just save both of us some trouble. I know you're cheating on me. And if you were going to end up being like this, you could've left me alone that day in the airport."

"What are you talking about?"

"You've changed. There's no more passion in this relationship. It's like you're forcing yourself to even be around me. And I don't deserve that."

"You don't understand," Michael responded with the smallest amount of energy.

"Well, what exactly is there for me to make sense of, Michael? One minute we're lying in the bed discussing how we can't live without each other, and the next minute, you're barely here and we're not even having sex anymore. It's all pretty clear to me what's going on."

"Please! Stop talking and listen to me for just one moment." Slightly raising his voice and reining in his frustration, he began to speak again. "There is something that I haven't told you about me. I've kept this from you to protect you, but at this moment, it seems I can no longer go on with this secret in my mind and my heart. It's weighing me down, and now it's weighing you down."

Desirae moved to the edge of her seat. "Michael, I'm not about to sit here and allow you to tell me that I have been spending all of my time with a married man. Silly me for believing that a guy like you would be any different from the rest of them." She stood in preparation to storm out of the room when Michael grabbed her wrist.

"I'm sick," he whispered under his breath.

"What did you just say?"

"I said I'm sick, Desirae. Now if you would just sit down for a moment and allow me to get a word in this conversation, I can explain."

Stunned, Desirae fell back into her seat at the table. She looked deeply into Michael's eyes, giving him her undivided attention as he spoke.

"About four years ago, I was diagnosed with a rare form of brain cancer. There were no indications. As you know, I eat well, exercise regularly, and take overall good care of myself. The doctors said that there was nothing I could have done differently to avoid this. And when I received the diagnosis, our firm was on the brink of winning the case against Logan & Logan."

"You mean the multimillion-dollar lawsuit that you're most known for?" Desirae interjected.

"Exactly. I didn't even know that I was sick. A routine doctor's visit and normal lab work determined abnormal cells. For at least a year after the diagnosis, I pretended that it didn't exist, hoping that it was a bad dream and that I'd one day wake up. That was until I worked relentlessly to the point of hospitalization."

"I remember that. I think the word amongst the attorneys was that you suffered from dehydration."

"Exactly. That's what I wanted everyone to know, and that was the story I gave."

Desirae, dazed and confused, made an attempt at an apology. "Michael, I am so very sorry. I had no idea that you were going through so much." She began to cry. "And look at me. Here I am, accusing you of horrible things when you're dealing with something so massive. I'm so sorry for assuming and not taking the time to listen to you."

Michael consoled her. "It's not your fault. You had no way of knowing. And I don't blame you for assuming the worst. You've been hurt before, and I know that. This is why I had to come forward and tell you this now."

"So has it been there this entire time?"

"No, I had several major surgeries years ago and it eventually went into remission. I found a few weeks ago that it was back and immediately started treatment."

"What kind of treatment?"

"Chemotherapy and radiation."

"Okay, what happens now? I mean, did the doctors say if there is a way to heal you completely this time?"

"Unfortunately, this can't be reversed, and there is no way to predict where things might go from here. The way I see it, life never gives us a guarantee of time. Not one of us is guaranteed time on this earth. About a year ago, I resolved to live every day as though it were my last. When you came into my life, you reminded me of how sweet life could be, and you gave me something to look forward to. Selfishly, this is why I've wanted to spend every day with you. I have to be honest with you; I don't know what may change or stay the same about my life. The only thing that I know for sure is how I feel about you. Unfortunately, this is a part of me that is not going away, at least for now. So before you go making decisions to spend the rest of your life with me, it's only fair that you know what that could look like."

Desirae sat in silence as tears flowed from her eyes, which Michael tried to wipe away. "Desirae, I also want you to know that should you decide to walk away from all of this, I won't blame you one bit. You have your whole life ahead of you. So, for today, let's just enjoy this moment because it is what's promised to us."

Desirae leaned on Michael's chest and sobbed. "I'm not leaving you. I'm going to be by your side. There is nothing that you're going to go through alone. You have been my rock this entire time, and now it's time for me to be that for you."

You're All I Need to Get By

Standing at her car, Ashlee was forced to acknowledge the sweltering heat while adding what she believed to be the last of the items to the trunk. "Nolan, do you have anything else to go in the car before we hit the road?"

Her father appeared at the threshold of the front door. "And if he does have anything else, I can't imagine where it might go," he said sarcastically.

"Now don't start with me, Daddy. I'm preparing to get on the road to go to a family reunion that you technically could be attending as well."

"Technically, my ass. You know good and well that I have no intention of traveling to any city that your momma is in, let alone set foot in the same house. Oh no." He flailed his arms in the air.

Ashlee sighed and rolled her eyes.

"Grandpa is funny," said Nolan as he approached the door with a small duffle bag.

"You've got that right, baby; your grandpa is very funny. As a matter of fact, he tells jokes regularly."

As Nolan exited the house, a car circled the driveway before pulling in.

"Daddy!" Nolan shouted with joy.

"And will you look at who decided to make an entrance?" Ashlee questioned. "Xavier, what are you doing here?"

Xavier exited the car with a bag of snacks in tow. "Now you already know that I was not about to let my son get on the road without bringing him some snacks."

"Let me take a look at what's in that bag. And I do hope that by snacks, you don't mean candy." As Ashlee walked toward Nolan, he snatched the bag closed and motioned for Nolan to come and retrieve it from him.

"Well, there may be a little of that in there too."

"I knew it," squealed Ashlee.

Nolan plunged into his father's arms while reaching for the bag.

Cynthia now came to the front of the house with her carry-on luggage. "Babe, here is the last thing that I need to put in the car."

"Looks like you are planning to stay for a whole week," Ashlee's father scoffed.

"I doubt we'll be there that long based on what I've heard," she replied.

"You've got that right."

"Besides, I've got to get back to work on Monday morning, so I know that this is only a weekend trip for us."

Ashlee interjected, "Speaking of work, I have to drop off this picnic basket I made this morning to Will before we actually get on the highway. It shouldn't take us long."

"Cool, well if you are ready, then so are we."

Ashlee made her rounds to give hugs. "See you later, Dad. Please behave while we are gone." She pointed her fingers toward her eyes and back to him, letting him know she was watching him as she walked over to Xavier, still hugging Nolan. "We'll see you when we get back as well."

"You got it. Please drive safely and know that I'm just a phone call away, should you guys need anything. Take care of my boy."

Once in the car, Cynthia expressed gratitude that Ashlee's father had been so easygoing with the two dating.

"Well, I'm not surprised. My dad has known about me for years, but you're the first woman that he has seen me with. It's my mom that I'm worried about."

"Well, we will see soon," Cynthia responded to comfort Ashlee.

As they drove up the winding road of trees leading to Will's house, two bodies were standing outside waving them toward the entrance. A closer glance revealed Will and his girlfriend arm in arm waiting to greet Ashlee and her family.

As Ashlee pulled the car into the driveway and placed it in park, she hopped out and passed the basket to Will while extending her arms to hug his girlfriend, and then turned to Will. "At the last event, you were introducing me to the love of your life, now it's my turn to introduce both of you to the love of my life." She motioned for Cynthia to get out of the car and join her. "Nolan, you come too!"

They both got out of the car and greeted Will and his girlfriend.

"Wow, little man, you are growing like wildfire. I know your daddy is going to have you playing football or basketball real soon." Ashlee rolled her eyes at Will. "Cynthia, please meet my lady Nadia."

They all exchanged pleasantries and Ashlee noticed that Cynthia looked as if she'd seen a ghost.

Will's inquiry broke up the moment. "By the way, Ash, how did the two of you meet?"

Ashlee and Cynthia looked at each other, and Ashlee said, "I'll take this one, babe. So we were in college and studying partners who found love and friendship amidst the books. And before you ask, she's the smart one, I just do my best to keep up over here." Ashlee grinned. "Anyway, we all have to get going so please enjoy this picnic basket and your date. We're preparing to hit the road."

"Well, it was a pleasure meeting you, Cynthia," said Will with a tremendous smile on his face. "Nolan, take it, easy young man. Here's a little something for you," he added in a whisper as he slid Nolan a twenty-dollar bill behind everyone's back.

Cynthia replied, "It was a pleasure meeting you all as well."

They all said their goodbyes, and Ashlee, Cynthia, and Nolan walked to the car.

Once inside, Ashlee noticed that Cynthia was quieter than usual. With the drive ahead in mind, Ashlee set the music, placed the car in reverse to get out of the driveway, and they departed. "So, are you going to tell me what's wrong with you? Since we left Will's spot, you haven't been the same."

Cynthia turned to Ashlee. "You really want to know?"

"Uh, yeah. I really want to know," Ashlee confirmed.

"Well, that wasn't my first time meeting Will's girlfriend. I've met her before."

Now concerned, Ashlee responded, "Met her how?"

"After I graduated, I started hanging out with two ladies from my job. It was like I made an instant connection with them because they were the only few Black women there. You already know how corporations can be. I later found out that they were lesbians. And the way I learned was that they invited me to a houseparty that they threw often. When I got there, I was surprised to be in the company of so many women like us. Babe, these women were strong and confident and seemingly not running away from their truths."

"Yeah, but I don't get what all of this has to do with Will's girl."

"That's the kicker, she was a longtime girlfriend of one of the hosts. And if I'm not mistaken, they may still even be together, but I'm not a hundred percent sure on that part. All I know is that she is lying in a bed of untruths. Seeing her standing with Will proclaiming to be in love shook me."

"Damn, Will would be distraught if he were to find out. He has made it clear that he is in love with her. I feel so bad for him. Are you sure she's the same person?"

"I'm one hundred percent sure. And the thought of someone not being fully who they are and lying on a bed of lies drives me insane."

"Well, baby, you don't have anything to worry about."

"Speaking of the truth, I need to know that I'm not just coming on this trip as a sideshow."

Ashlee turned to look her in the eyes. "Babe, you could never be a sideshow. I would never disrespect you like that. Come on now."

"Okay, if you say so," she said as she reached for Ashlee's hand and turned to the window, allowing the sun to shine on her face.

"You're not a sideshow. I've told you how my mom is, so I cannot guarantee how she will respond to seeing you."

They continued to drive for hours on the highway. Between singing songs and a few movies, the time passed by quickly. When they reached their destination, Ashlee was noticeably emotional but worked to hide it from Nolan. Cynthia gently stroked her neck, recognizing that this was the home that Ashlee grew up in.

"This place is filled with so many memories. I just hope I can get through the time here."

"You will be just fine. You know that I've got your back."

"Mommy, can we see Granny now?"

"Of course, let me get you out. I'll come back to get our things in just a bit."

Ashlee allowed Nolan to run to the front door, but it opened before he could knock.

"Grandma!" Nolan yelled and squeezed her tight.

"Hello, Momma. We made it!" Ashlee exclaimed from the distance. Several family members rushed over to greet Ashlee and Nolan, a few wondering and whispering about who was accompanying them.

Ashlee exchanged a prolonged hug with her mother before introducing Cynthia. "Momma, this is my friend Cynthia."

Cutting her eyes and allowing a faint "Hello. Nice to meet you" escape her lips, Ashlee's mother was noticeably disapproving. Ashlee ignored the signs and began introducing Cynthia to her other family members. "Babe, meet Aunt Ida, and over here is her husband Uncle James." Pointing to the left and right of the room as they entered the house, Ashlee presented her family members one by one.

Offended amidst the introductions lacking truth, Cynthia cornered Ashlee for a private discussion. "Babe, I need to talk to you. Now I know that I promised to come on this trip with you and to be by your side through it all, but I'm sick and tired of you not fully disclosing the truth and people acting as if I'm forcing you to be something that you're not. I feel like people around here are staring at me like I'm responsible for your being gay, and we all know that's not the truth."

"Of course not. And I never said anything like that."

"Yeah, but the judgment around here tells a different story. At the end of the day, I am only concerned with one person, and that is your mother. When do you plan to tell her?"

"You mean to tell her what she already knows?"

"I mean tell her that you are gay and that we are together."

"At this point, is it really necessary?" Ashlee inquired.

"It's necessary. It's the thing that tore us apart before. If you can't make a commitment to me by telling your mom about us, I can no longer pretend that I will be okay with it. And I told you that day in the coffee shop that I was not here to play with love."

"Wait, can we talk about this?"

"There is nothing left to talk about. Either you tell your mother about us, or you and I are done. Now, if you will excuse me, I'm going to go over here and find myself a quiet seat on that couch, next to one of your cousins, and you can let me know when you figure it out." She walked away in confirmation of her words.

Ashlee, now petrified, snuck into the bathroom to make a call to the only person that she knew could help her make sense of the situation. After dialing the number, she placed the phone to her ear and waited impatiently for an answer. "Pickup, pickup, pickup," she murmured.

"What's up, Ash?"

"Man, listen. I'm caught between a rock and a hard place. Cynthia is telling me that if I don't tell my mom about us while we're here, that she is going to end the relationship for good. I can't lose her again, I just can't. And you already know how my momma is."

The voice on the other end of the phone was familiar and comforting. "Listen to me, Ash, it's time for you to live for you. What others think about you has had too much control over you and it has held you hostage. It's time to break free. You deserve to be free."

"Yes, that sounds nice and all, but how do I do that?" Ashlee heard her mother yelling from the other room. "Hey, I have to go, I hear yelling and that's never a good thing. I'll call you back." She hung up the phone and rushed into her mother's room, where she found Nolan standing at his grandmother's dresser while her mother sat on the bed. "Momma, what's wrong? Did something happen? Is everything okay?"

Her mother turned around with a striking stare and looked at Ashlee. "Ashlee, this boy says that lady you brought here with you is living at your house. He said that she is your girlfriend. I know that your father is a foolish man, but I can't imagine him standing for allowing you to poison this boy's mind with this type of behavior."

Fed up, Ashlee began to speak. "That's just it, Momma, it's not poison to be who you are. I've been trying for the life of me to tell you who I was. For as long as I can remember I've been trying to get you to see me."

"Girl, what in heaven's name are you talking about? I have always seen you. I saw you when you wanted to stop wearing the dresses with the lace. I saw you when you wanted to play outside with the boys instead of inside with the girls. I saw you when you wanted to play sports and work up there at that gym. I even saw you when you wanted to go in another direction after graduating from college. Truth is, I've always seen you and known about who you were."

With tears streaming down her face, Ashlee attempted to express herself. "Well, Momma, if you knew, why didn't you tell me? How come you never accepted me for who I was? I was never fully myself around you because you didn't allow me to be."

Her mother frowned in response. "Aw. Don't try to blame me for your demons. Those are your demons, not mine. I tried to give you a better life than that. Do you think I want my child to have to struggle being judged by strangers every day? I never wanted that for you. Life is hard for people who are gay. Why would anyone ever choose that lifestyle? I don't understand it."

"That's just it, Momma. This isn't a choice, it's just who I am. And I am no longer afraid to say that Cynthia and I are together. We hope to get married someday. We will raise Nolan together and maybe even have more kids in the future. This is who I am, Momma, and I'm just hoping that you will accept me as I am." Ashlee, sobbing, walked over to kneel at her mother's feet.

"Momma, can you take me as I am?"

Rubbing the top of Ashlee's hair, she replied "I'm sorry, baby, I don't think I can."

Ashlee shed one last series of tears and used her sleeve to wipe her face before standing up and saying, "Well then, I guess we don't belong here. I'm sorry we ever came. Nolan, get your bag. We're leaving."

Ashlee walked to the couch in search of Cynthia, but to no avail. She looked in each of the bedrooms with closed doors unsuccessfully and then walked outside, but Cynthia was nowhere to be found.

Ashlee's cousin Brittany stepped outside. "If you're looking for Cynthia, she left. She told me to tell you goodbye."

Ashlee dropped to her knees in tears.

FML

"Hey, baby. I'm about to run to the store real quick," Derek shouted as he exited the front door. As he settled in the car, he received several text messages from Rebecca. It had been a few weeks since the run-in at the grocery store, and he had continued to avoid her since.

> *Derek, I know you're getting my messages. I'm five months now and you're still avoiding me and this baby. We need to talk to figure out what the future will look like. I understand that you're staying with your wife, but we need to be able to at least co-parent amicably. You're going to make me do something I don't want to do if you do not call me now.*

Derek deleted the message and continued to pull out of the garage to go run his errands.

Inside, Jennifer called to talk to her mom.

"Have you guys heard anything about the results of the treatments? Do I have a grandbaby yet?"

"No, Mom, as of right now we haven't heard anything. You have to be patient."

"Yes, yes, I know. But it's so hard to not be a little anxious."

"I understand. I'm trying to not think about it too much or I will drive myself crazy."

"How's Derek?"

"Oh, he's great. He just left to go run some errands before we take the pregnancy test tonight."

"Oh, well, call me soon as you guys know either way."

"I will. I have been thinking a lot more about the writing I've been doing."

"Okay, what about it?"

"I've decided to stop writing altogether."

There was silence on the phone as Jennifer's mom tried to find the words to respond. "Well, I am a little surprised by the decision. You have always been so firm with me that it was something that you could never walk away from fully. So what changed your mind?"

Jennifer heard a car pull into the driveway, so she got up from the sofa to go see who it could be. "Mom, after everything that has gone on these last couple of months between Derek and me, it has put things in perspective. Just the idea that I kept it a secret of how hard I was trying to conceive eventually caused a lot of tension in the relationship. I just think it's best to put the writing to the side for a while and focus solely on my family."

"I can understand that, dear. Sometimes you do have to make sacrifices for your family."

"Hey, Ma, I'm going to call you back, someone is at the door."

The two hung up and Jennifer looked out the window, puzzled as to why Rebecca was at her home.

The doorbell rang and she quickly made her way to answer it.

"Hi, Jennifer, how are you?"

"I'm great. Can I help you with something?"

"Yes, you can. Do you mind if I come in?"

"Sure," Jennifer said while opening the door and warmly motioning her to enter the home. They walked to the living room, where Jennifer offered Rebecca tea while turning off the television.

"Oh, no I'm okay. Thanks for offering."

"Of course, no problem. You've grown a lot since I saw you. Do you know what you're having?"

"Yes, a boy."

"That's exciting! I'm sure the dad is ecstatic."

Rebecca gave a half-smile while shuffling in her chair in an attempt to find the right angle to provide comfort to her back. "Well, I know you're wondering what I'm doing here."

"Yes, I'm curious. That and how you knew where we lived."

Ignoring the latter, Rebecca responded, "I needed to have a conversation with you, one that is hard to have."

"Okay, what is it?"

"I want you to know that I'm coming to you as a woman and that I meant you no disrespect. There's honestly no excuse for my behavior."

"Girl, spit it out."

"I've been sleeping with Derek for over a year now."

In disbelief, Jennifer let out a burst of laughter, which frightened Rebecca. "I'm laughing because you clearly do not know me to think that's a good joke to play."

"I'm not joking."

Jennifer dropped the glass of juice she had been drinking, shattering it on the floor. She stormed out of the room into the nearby guest room, shutting the door behind her. She paced the room, trying to decide if she should even believe this crazy bitch or whether she should call Derek now. She became more infuriated thinking about moments that had passed that didn't feel right, but she'd ignored it. Derek leaving the other day randomly, the grocery store encounter. If anything, Jennifer now needed answers before Derek returned. She gathered herself and reentered the living room.

"To be clear, the only reason I haven't beat your ass yet is that you're pregnant."

Not surprised by the statement, Rebecca caressed her stomach with her hands once, realizing it was her shield.

"I'm assuming you're here talking to me because Derek is not giving you the fairytale ending you wanted."

"Yes, he's been ignoring my calls and texts. But I'm not trying to be with him anymore. I just want him to step up and be a father to his child. I've accepted what the situation has become. I promise I'm not trying to cause you or your family any more hurt than I already have."

"Did you really think he was going to leave his home for you? How dumb could you be? Furthermore, you had the nerve to play nice in my face at the store knowing you were fucking my man. You're getting exactly what you deserve. You're pathetic! All the men in the world but you were happy getting nothing-ass seconds with my man. How little you must think of yourself."

Rebecca remained silent, partially feeling humiliated and also understanding that Jennifer had every right to feel the way she did. Realizing that Rebecca was not going to give her a fight, Jennifer remembered her original reason for wanting to continue the conversation. "Tell me everything. When did you tell him you were pregnant?"

"The day I saw you guys at the grocery store."

"His response?"

"Nothing. He never responded, and I haven't heard from him since."

"When was the last time you had sex with him?"

"Weeks ago. It's been a while."

"Were y'all wearing condoms?"

"In the beginning, yes, but we soon after stopped."

"Whose idea was it to stop?"

"It was his, but he always pulled out."

Jennifer continued for minutes as an investigator, trying to obtain all the information she could before he returned. She knew Derek, and clearly by his actions, he would be far from forthcoming. And in Jennifer's favor, Rebecca was very helpful with every question that she had. Jennifer was internally heartbroken and could feel a deep pit in her stomach, but she refused to let Rebecca see how much pain she had caused.

Just as Rebecca was preparing to provide receipts for accusations, they were interrupted by keys rattling at the front door. They both took a deep breath and turned to greet Derek as he entered the house.

Derek walked into the living room to see both women standing, obviously waiting for his arrival. He dropped the groceries from his hand and remained speechless, for he did not know how much Rebecca had told Jennifer.

KEYS

We are not by-products of what happens to us, we are the women we choose to become in spite of it all.

— D.L.

Although at times, life paints a mirage of disorganization and disarray, the universe has no missing pieces. Each of us is assigned with a place and a purpose. To this end, there is a greater calling on our lives. Whether standing in the gap for loved ones, or broadening the horizons of what will be, every step that we take has deeper meaning. And when we resolve to be present for those whom we love, our lives are shaped and molded divinely.

The friendship that Desirae, Ashlee and Jennifer dared to exchange lives and breathes and thrives among us. Often governed by a society that imposes unrealistic standards and imagery that don't reflect or depict the vast array of our existence, we often fail to recognize the necessity for belonging and the need for safe spaces from which to confront trauma of the past as well as present. When we resolve to fellowship and remain loyal to the bonds assigned to our lives, we bear witness to lives that fit together like missing pieces to a puzzle. These are the Pieces of Us.

181

ABOUT THE AUTHOR

Danielle Latrice is an author, screenwriter, and enthusiast for self-love and healing; whose purpose is to help emotionally distressed women that are in a vulnerable space to reclaim their peace by providing clarity and motivation to navigate their own journey of healing emotional scars and nurturing self-love. An Alabama native, she is a lover of naps, music, reading, and Alabama football, currently residing in Atlanta, most likely multitasking. Often describing herself as a collector of thoughts and possessing a gentle soul, she enjoys incorporating some of her life experiences and advocating for self-discovery, healing, self-love, and sisterhood in her fictional writing.

Her initial interest in writing started in middle school to which she shared through short stories with classmates, that would resurface at the age of 25. Over the years, she'd worked diligently at receiving a Bachelor of Science in Psychology and a Master of Science in Clinical Mental Health Counseling. The experience was illuminating for her personal growth, but she soon discovered, it would not be the route planned to fulfill her life's purpose. The combination of her education and the life experiences that left emotional scars and built an emptiness of self-love all nurtured her strong belief in the pursuit of personal healing. She does not consider herself to be an expert but simply traveling her own journey of healing.

Over the next few years, she looks forward to producing a web series that's based upon the novel, with the long-term goal to bring that and other projects to television to capture a much larger audience. As an extension of the book, she will be releasing self-guided healing cards and launching the She's Pieced Together organization, a community of women that's based on love, support, inspiration, and reciprocity.

CONNECT WITH DANIELLE LATRICE ON SOCIAL MEDIA

Website:	www.daniellelatrice.com
Email:	info@daniellelatrice.com
IG:	danni_latrice_
Twitter:	danni_latrice_
Facebook:	Danielle Latrice
Youtube:	Danielle Latrice

AFFIRMATION CARDS

The Pieced Together Self-Guided Healing Cards are 31 days of affirmation, guidance, and manifestation. Daily affirmations and associated tasks provided to help establish a foundation to start a journey of self-discovery, healing, and self-love. The cards are not designed to serve as the ultimate remedy, but a starting point for nurturing self-love, healing emotional scars, and manifesting a vibrant future.